GRIMM'S FAIRY TALES

Jacob and Wilhelm Grimm

SCHOLASTIC INC.

ISBN 978-0-545-93490-9

10 9 8 7 6 5 4 3 2 1   16 17 18 19 20

Printed in the U.S.A.   40
First printing 2016

Contents

Hansel and Gretel

HARD BY A GREAT FOREST dwelt a poor woodcutter with his wife and his two children. The boy was called Hansel and the girl Gretel. The woodcutter had little to bite and to break, and once when great scarcity fell on the land, he could no longer procure daily bread. Now, when he thought over this by night in his bed, and tossed about in his anxiety, he groaned and said to his wife, "What is to become of us? How are we to feed our poor children, when we no longer have anything even for ourselves?"

"I'll tell you what, husband," answered the woman, "Early tomorrow morning we will take the children out into the forest to where it is the thickest; there we will light a fire for them and give each of them one piece of bread more, and then we will go to our work and leave them alone. They will not find the way home again, and we shall be rid of them."

"No, wife," said the man. "I will not do that; how can I bear to leave my children alone in the forest? The wild animals would soon come and tear them to pieces."

"O, thou fool!" said she. "Then we must all four die of hunger; thou mayest as well plane the planks for our coffins," and she left him no peace until he consented.

"But I feel very sorry for the poor children, all the same," said the man.

The two children had also not been able to sleep for hunger, and had heard what their stepmother had said to their father. Gretel wept bitter tears and said to Hansel, "Now all is over with us."

"Be quiet, Gretel," said Hansel. "Do not distress thyself, I will soon find a way to help us." And when the old folks had fallen asleep, he got up, put on his little coat, opened the door below, and crept outside. The moon shone brightly, and the white pebbles that lay in front of the house glittered like real silver pennies. Hansel stooped and put as many of them in the little pocket of his coat as he could possibly get in. Then he went back and said to Gretel, "Be comforted, dear little sister, and sleep in peace; God will not forsake us," and he lay down again in his bed.

When day dawned, but before the sun had risen, the woman came and awoke the two children, saying, "Get up, you sluggards! We are going into the forest to fetch wood." She gave each a little piece of bread and said, "There is something for your dinner, but do not eat it up before then, for you will get nothing else." Gretel took the bread under her apron, as Hansel had the stones in his pocket. Then they all set out together on the way to the forest.

When they had walked a short time, Hansel stood still and peeped back at the house, and did so again and again. His father said, "Hansel, what art thou looking at there and staying behind for? Mind what thou art about, and do not forget how to use thy legs."

"Ah, Father," said Hansel, "I am looking at my little white cat, which is sitting up on the roof and wants to say good-bye to me."

The wife said, "Fool, that is not thy little cat; that is the morning sun shining on the chimneys." Hansel, however, had not been looking back at the cat, but had been constantly throwing one of the white pebbles out of his pocket on the road.

When they had reached the middle of the forest, the father said, "Now, children, pile up some wood, and I will light a fire so that you may not be cold."

Hansel and Gretel gathered brushwood together, as high as a little hill. The brushwood was lighted, and when the flames were burning very high, the woman said, "Now, children, lay yourselves down by the fire and rest; we will go into the forest and cut some wood. When we have done, we will come back and fetch you away."

Hansel and Gretel sat by the fire, and when noon

came, each ate a little piece of bread, and as they heard the strokes of the wood axe they believed that their father was near. It was not, however, the axe— it was a branch that he had fastened to a withered tree, which the wind was blowing backward and forward. And as they had been sitting such a long time, their eyes shut with fatigue, and they fell fast asleep. When at last they awoke, it was already dark night. Gretel began to cry and said, "How are we to get out of the forest now?"

But Hansel comforted her and said, "Just wait a little, until the moon has risen, and then we will soon find the way." When the full moon had risen, Hansel took his little sister by the hand and followed the pebbles, which shone like newly coined silver pieces, and showed them the way.

They walked the whole night long, and by break of day came once more to their father's house. They knocked at the door, and when the woman opened it and saw that it was Hansel and Gretel, she said, "You naughty children, why have you slept so long in the forest? We thought you were never coming back at all!" The father, however, rejoiced, for it had cut him to the heart to leave them behind alone.

Not long afterward, there was once more great scarcity in all parts, and the children heard their stepmother saying at night to their father, "Everything is eaten again; we have one half loaf left, and after that there is an end. The children must go. We will take them farther into the woods so that they will not find their way out again; there is no other means of saving ourselves!"

The man's heart was heavy, and he said, "It would be better for thee to share the last mouthful with thy children." The woman, however, would listen to nothing that he had to say, but scolded and reproached him. He who says A must say B, likewise, and as he had yielded the first time, he had to do so a second time also.

The children were, however, still awake and had heard the conversation. When the old folks were asleep, Hansel again got up and wanted to go out and pick up pebbles as he had done before—but the woman had locked the door, and Hansel could not get out. Nevertheless, he comforted his little sister and said, "Do not cry, Gretel. Go to sleep quietly; the good God will help us."

Early in the morning the woman came and took the children out of their beds. Their bit of bread was given to them, but it was smaller still than the time before. On the way into the forest, Hansel crumbled his in his pocket and often stood still and threw a morsel on the ground. "Hansel, why dost thou stop and look round?" said the father. "Go on."

"I am looking back at my little pigeon, which is sitting on the roof and wants to say good-bye to me," answered Hansel.

"Simpleton!" said the woman. "That is not thy little pigeon, that is the morning sun shining on the chimney." Hansel, however, little by little, threw all the crumbs on the path.

The woman led the children deeper still into the forest, where they had never in their lives been before. Then a great fire was again made, and the stepmother said, "Just sit there, you children, and when you are tired you may sleep a little; we are going into the forest to cut wood, and in the evening when we are done, we will come and fetch you away."

When it was noon, Gretel shared her piece of bread with Hansel, who had scattered his along the way. Then they fell asleep and evening came and went, but no one came to the poor children. They did not awake until it was dark night, and Hansel comforted his little sister and said, "Just wait, Gretel, until the moon rises, and then we shall see the crumbs of bread that I have strewn about; they will show us our way home again." When the moon came they set out, but they found no crumbs, for the many thousands of birds that fly about in the woods and fields had picked them all up. Hansel said to Gretel, "We shall soon find the way," but they did not find it. They walked the whole night and all the next day, too, from morning till evening, but they did not get out of the forest, and were very hungry, for they had nothing to eat but two or three berries that grew on the ground. And as they were so weary that their legs would carry them no longer, they lay down beneath a tree and fell asleep.

It was now three mornings since they had left their father's house. They began to walk again, but they always got deeper into the forest, and if help did not come soon, they must die of hunger and weariness. When it was midday, they saw a beautiful snow-white bird sitting on a bough, which sang so delightfully that they stood still and listened to it. And when it had finished its song, it spread its wings and flew away before them, and they followed it until they reached a little house, on the roof of which it landed; and when they came up to the little house they saw that it was built of bread and covered with cakes, but that the windows were of clear sugar. "We will set to work on that," said Hansel, "and have a good meal. I will eat a bit of the roof, and thou, Gretel, canst eat some of the window; it will taste sweet." Hansel reached up above and broke off a little of the roof to try how it tasted, and Gretel leaned against the window and nibbled at the panes.

Then a soft voice cried from the room,

"Nibble, nibble, gnaw,
Who is nibbling at my little house?"

The children answered,

"The wind, the wind,
The heaven-born wind,"

and went on eating without disturbing themselves. Hansel, who thought the roof tasted very nice, tore down a great piece of it, and Gretel pushed out the whole of one round windowpane, sat down, and enjoyed herself with it. Suddenly the door opened, and a very, very old woman, who supported herself on crutches, came creeping out. Hansel and Gretel were so terribly frightened that they let fall what they had in their hands. The old woman, however, nodded her head and said, "Oh, you dear children, who has brought you here? Do come in, and stay with me. No harm shall happen to you." She took them both by the hand and led them into her little house. Then good food was set before them: milk and pancakes, with sugar, apples, and nuts. Afterward, two pretty little beds were covered with clean white linen, and Hansel and Gretel lay down in them and thought they were in heaven.

The old woman had only pretended to be so kind; she was in reality a wicked witch, who lay in wait for children and had only built the little house of bread in order to entice them there. When a child fell into her power, she killed, cooked, and ate it, and that was a feast day with her. Witches have red eyes and cannot see far, but they have a keen scent like the beasts and are aware when human beings draw near. When Hansel and Gretel came into her neighborhood, she laughed maliciously, and said mockingly, "I have them; they shall not escape me again!"

Early in the morning before the children were awake, she was already up, and when she saw both of them sleeping and looking so pretty, with their plump red cheeks, she muttered to herself, "That will be a dainty mouthful!" Then she seized Hansel with her shriveled hand, carried him into a little stable, and shut him in with a grated door. He might scream as he liked, but that was of no use. Then she went to Gretel, shook her till she awoke, and cried, "Get up, lazy thing, fetch some water, and cook something good for thy brother. He is in the stable outside and is to be made fat. When he is fat, I will eat him." Gretel began to weep bitterly, but it was all in vain; she was forced to do what the wicked witch ordered her.

And now the best food was cooked for poor Hansel, but Gretel got nothing but crab shells. Every morning, the woman crept to the little stable and cried, "Hansel, stretch out thy finger, that I may feel if thou wilt soon be fat." Hansel, however, stretched out a little bone to her, and the old woman, who had dim eyes, could not see it. She thought it was Hansel's finger, and was astonished that there was no way of fattening him. When four weeks had gone by, and Hansel still continued to be thin, she was seized with impatience and would not wait any longer. "Hello, Gretel," she cried to the girl. "Be active, and bring some water. Let Hansel be fat or lean, tomorrow I will kill him and cook him."

Ah, how the poor little sister did lament when she had to fetch the water, and how her tears did flow down over her cheeks! "Dear God, do help us," she cried. "If the wild beasts in the forest had but devoured us, we should at any rate have died together."

"Just keep thy noise to thyself," said the old woman. "All that won't help thee at all."

Early in the morning, Gretel had to go out and hang up the cauldron with the water and light the fire. "We will bake first," said the old woman. "I have already heated the oven and kneaded the dough." She pushed poor Gretel out to the oven, from which flames of fire were already darting. "Creep in," said the witch, "and see if it is properly heated so that we can shut the bread in." And once Gretel was inside, the witch intended to shut the oven and let her bake in it, and then she would eat her, too.

But Gretel saw what she had in her mind and said,

"I do not know how I am to do it; how do you get in?"

"Silly goose," said the old woman, "the door is big enough; just look, I can get in myself!" and she crept up and thrust her head into the oven. Then Gretel gave her a push that drove her far into it, shut the iron door, and fastened the bolt. Oh! Then she began to howl quite horribly, but Gretel ran away, and the witch was miserably burnt to death.

Gretel, however, ran like lightning to Hansel, opened his little stable, and cried, "Hansel, we are saved! The old witch is dead!" Then Hansel sprang out like a bird from its cage when the door is opened for it. How they did rejoice and embrace each other, and dance about and kiss each other! And as they had no longer any need to fear her, they went into the witch's house, and in every corner there stood chests full of pearls and jewels.

"These are far better than pebbles!" Hansel said, and thrust into his pockets whatever could be got in.

Gretel said, "I, too, will take something home with me," and filled her pinafore full.

"But now we will go away," said Hansel, "that we may get out of the witch's forest."

When they had walked for two hours, they came to a great piece of water. "We cannot get over," said Hansel. "I see no foot-plank, and no bridge."

"And no boat crosses, either," answered Gretel. "But a white duck is swimming there; if I ask her, she will help us over." Then she cried,

> "Little duck, little duck, dost thou see,
> Hansel and Gretel are waiting for thee?
> There's never a plank, or bridge in sight,
> Take us across on thy back so white."

The duck came to them, and Hansel seated himself on its back and told his sister to sit by him. "No," replied Gretel, "that will be too heavy for the little duck; she shall take us across, one after the other." The good little duck did so, and once they were safely across and had walked for a short time, the forest seemed to be more and more familiar to them, and at length they saw from afar their father's house. Then they began to run, rushed into the parlor, and threw themselves into their father's arms. The man had not known one happy hour since he had left the children in the forest; the woman, however, was dead. Gretel emptied her pinafore until pearls and precious stones ran about the room, and Hansel threw one handful after another out of his pocket to add to them. Then all anxiety was at an end, and they lived together in perfect happiness.

My tale is done—there runs a mouse; whosoever catches it may make a big fur cap out of it.

Iron John

THERE WAS ONCE UPON A TIME a king who had a great forest near his palace, full of all kinds of wild animals. One day he sent out a huntsman to shoot him a doe, but he did not come back. "Perhaps some accident has befallen him," said the king, and the next day he sent out two more huntsmen who were to search for him, but they, too, stayed away. Then on the third day, he sent for all his huntsmen, and said, "Scour the whole forest through, and do not give up until ye have found all three." But of these, also, none came home again, and of the pack of hounds that they had taken with them, none were seen more. From that time forth, no one would any longer venture into the forest, and it lay there in deep stillness and solitude, and nothing was seen of it, but sometimes an eagle or a hawk flying over it.

This lasted for many years, when a strange huntsman announced himself to the king as seeking work, and offered to go into the dangerous forest. The king, however, would not give his consent, and said, "It is not safe in there; I fear it would fare with thee no better than with the others, and thou wouldst never come out again."

The huntsman replied, "Lord, I will venture it at my own risk. Of fear I know nothing."

The huntsman therefore betook himself with his dog to the forest. It was not long before the dog fell in with some game on the way and wanted to pursue it, but hardly had the dog run two steps when it stood before a deep pool, could go no farther, and a naked arm stretched itself out of the water, seized it, and drew it under. When the huntsman saw that, he went back and fetched three men to come with buckets and bail out the water. When they could see to the bottom, there lay a wild man whose body was brown like rusty iron, and whose hair hung over his face down to his knees. They bound him with cords and led him away to the castle. There was great astonishment over the wild man; the king, however, had him put in an iron cage in his courtyard, and forbade the door to be opened on pain of death, and the queen herself was to take the key into her keeping. From this time forth everyone could again go into the forest with safety.

The king had a son of eight years, who was once playing in the courtyard, and while he was playing, his golden ball fell into the cage. The boy ran thither and said, "Give me my ball out."

"Not till thou hast opened the door for me," answered the man.

"No," said the boy, "I will not do that; the king has forbidden it," and ran away.

The next day he again went and asked for his ball; the wild man said, "Open my door," but the boy would not.

On the third day the king had ridden out hunting, and the boy went once more and said, "I cannot open the door even if I wished, for I have not the key."

Then the wild man said, "It lies under thy mother's pillow; thou canst get it there." The boy, who wanted to have his ball back, cast all thought to the winds and brought the key. The door opened with difficulty, and the boy pinched his fingers. When it was open the wild man stepped out, gave him the golden ball, and hurried away.

The boy had become afraid; he called and cried after him, "Oh, wild man, do not go away, or I shall be beaten!" The wild man turned back, took him up, set him on his shoulder, and went with hasty steps into the forest. When the king came home, he observed the empty cage and asked the queen how that had happened. She knew nothing about it and sought the key, but it was gone. She called the boy, but no one answered. The king sent out people to seek for him in the fields, but they did not find him. Then he could easily guess what had happened, and much grief reigned in the royal court.

When the wild man had once more reached the dark forest, he took the boy down from his shoulder and said to him, "Thou wilt never see thy father and mother again, but I will keep thee with me, for thou hast set me free, and I have compassion on thee. If thou dost all I bid thee, thou shalt fare well. Of treasure and gold have I enough, and more than anyone in the world." He made a bed of moss for the boy on which he slept, and the next morning the man took him to a well and said, "Behold, the gold well is as bright and clear as crystal; thou shalt sit beside it, and take care that nothing falls into it, or it will be polluted. I will come every evening to see if thou hast obeyed my order."

The boy placed himself by the margin of the well and often saw a golden fish or a golden snake show itself therein, and took care that nothing fell in. As he was thus sitting, his finger hurt him so violently that he involuntarily put it in the water. He drew it quickly out again, but saw that it was quite gilded, and whatsoever pains he took to wash the gold off again, all was to no purpose. In the evening Iron John came back, looked at the boy, and said, "What has happened to the well?"

"Nothing, nothing," he answered, and held his finger behind his back so that the man might not see it.

But Iron John said, "Thou hast dipped thy finger into the water. This time it may pass, but take care thou dost not again let anything go in."

By daybreak the boy was already sitting by the well and watching it. His finger hurt him again and he passed it over his head, and then unhappily a hair fell down into the well. He took it quickly out, but it was already quite gilded. Iron John came and already knew what had happened. "Thou hast let a hair fall into the well," said he. "I will allow thee to watch by it once more, but if this happens for the third time, then the well is polluted, and thou canst no longer remain with me."

On the third day, the boy sat by the well and did not stir his finger, however much it hurt him. But the time was long to him, and he looked at the reflection of his face on the surface of the water. As he bent down more and more still while he was doing so, and trying to look straight into the eyes, his long hair fell down from his shoulders into the water. He raised himself up quickly, but the whole of the hair of his head was already golden and shone like the sun. You may imagine how terrified the poor boy was! He took his pocket handkerchief and tied it round his head, in order that the man might not see it.

When the man came he already knew everything and said, "Take the handkerchief off." Then the golden hair streamed forth, and though the boy excused himself as he might, it was of no use. "Thou hast not stood the trial, and canst stay here no longer. Go forth into the world; there thou wilt learn what poverty is. But as thou hast not a bad heart, and as I mean well by thee, there is one thing I will grant thee; if thou fallest into any difficulty, come to the forest and cry, 'Iron John,' and then I will come and help thee. My power is great, greater than thou thinkest, and I have gold and silver in abundance."

Then the king's son left the forest and walked by beaten and unbeaten paths ever onward until at length he reached a great city. There he looked for work, but could find none, and he had learnt nothing by which he could help himself. At length he went to the palace and asked if they would take him in. The people about the court did not at all know what use they could make of him, but they liked him and told him to stay. At length the cook took him into his service and said he might carry wood and water, and rake the cinders together.

Once when it so happened that no one else was at hand, the cook ordered him to carry the food to the royal table. But as he did not like to let his golden hair be seen, he kept his little cap on. Such a thing as that had never yet come under the king's notice, and he said, "When thou comest to the royal table, thou must take thy hat off."

The boy answered, "Ah, Lord, I cannot; I have a bad

sore place on my head." Then the king had the cook called before him and he scolded him and asked how he could take such a boy as that into his service; he ordered the cook to turn him off at once. The cook, however, had pity on him and exchanged him for the gardener's boy.

Now the boy had to plant and water the garden, hoe and dig, and bear the wind and bad weather. Once in summer when he was working alone in the garden, the day was so warm he took his little cap off so that the air might cool him. As the sun shone on his hair, it glittered and flashed so that the rays fell into the bedroom of the king's daughter, and up she sprang to see what that could be. Then she saw the boy and cried to him, "Boy, bring me a wreath of flowers."

He put his cap on with all haste, gathered wild field flowers, and bound them together. When he was ascending the stairs with them, the gardener met him and said, "How canst thou take the king's daughter a garland of such common flowers? Go quickly and get another, and seek out the prettiest and rarest."

"Oh, no," replied the boy, "the wild ones have more scent and will please her better."

When he got into the room, the king's daughter said, "Take thy cap off; it is not seemly to keep it on in my presence."

He again said, "I may not; I have a sore head." She, however, caught at his cap and pulled it off, and then his golden hair rolled down on his shoulders, and it was splendid to behold. He wanted to run out, but she held him by the arm and gave him a handful of ducats. With these he departed, but he cared nothing for the gold pieces. He took them to the gardener and said, "I present them to thy children, they can play with them." The following day the king's daughter again called to him that he was to bring her a wreath of field flowers, and when he went in with it, she instantly snatched at his cap and wanted to take it away from him, but he held it fast with both hands. She again gave him a handful of ducats, but he would not keep them and gave them to the gardener for playthings for his children. On the third day things went just the same; she could not get his cap away from him, and he would not have her money.

Not long afterward, the country was overrun by war. The king gathered together his people and did not know whether or not he could offer any opposition to the enemy, who was superior in strength and had a mighty army. Then said the gardener's boy, "I am grown up, and will go to the wars also. Only give me a horse."

The others laughed and said, "Seek one for thyself when we are gone; we will leave one behind us in the stable for thee." When they had gone forth, he went into the stable and got the horse out. It was lame of one foot and limped hobblety-jig, hobblety-jig; nevertheless, he mounted it and rode away to the dark forest.

When he came to the outskirts, he called "Iron John" three times, so loudly that it echoed through the trees. Thereupon the wild man appeared immediately and said, "What dost thou desire?"

"I want a strong steed, for I am going to the wars."

"That thou shalt have, and still more than thou askest for." Then the wild man went back into the forest, and it was not long before a stable boy came out of it, who led a horse that snorted with its nostrils and could hardly be restrained. Behind them followed a great troop of soldiers entirely equipped in iron and their swords flashed in the sun. The youth gave over his three-legged horse to the stable boy, mounted the other, and rode at the head of the soldiers.

When he got near the battlefield a great part of the king's men had already fallen, and little was wanting to make the rest give way. Then the youth galloped thither with his iron soldiers, broke like a hurricane over the enemy, and beat down all who opposed him. They began to fly, but the youth pursued, and never stopped, until there was not a single man left. Instead, however, of returning to the king, he conducted his troop via byways back to the forest and called forth Iron John.

"What dost thou desire?" asked the wild man.

"Take back thy horse and thy troops, and give me my three-legged horse again."

All that he asked was done, and soon he was riding on his three-legged horse. When the king returned to his palace, his daughter went to meet him and wished him joy of his victory. "I am not the one who carried away the victory," said he, "but a stranger knight who came to my assistance with his soldiers."

The daughter wanted to hear who the strange knight was, but the king did not know, and said, "He followed the enemy, and I did not see him again."

She inquired of the gardener where his boy was, but he smiled and said, "He has just come home on his three-legged horse, and the others have been mocking him and crying, 'Here comes our hobblety-jig back again!' They asked, too, 'Under what hedge hast thou been lying sleeping all the time?' He, however, said, 'I did the best of all, and it would have gone badly without me.' And then he was still more ridiculed."

The king said to his daughter, "I will proclaim a great feast that shall last for three days, and thou shalt throw a golden apple. Perhaps the unknown knight will come to it."

When the feast was announced, the youth went out

to the forest and called Iron John.

"What dost thou desire?" asked he.

"That I may catch the king's daughter's golden apple."

"It is as safe as if thou hadst it already," said Iron John. "Thou shalt likewise have a suit of red armor for the occasion, and ride on a spirited chestnut horse."

When the day came, the youth galloped to the spot, took his place among the knights, and was recognized by no one. The king's daughter came forward and threw a golden apple to the knights, but none of them caught it except he—only as soon as he had it, he galloped away.

On the second day, Iron John equipped him as a white knight and gave him a white horse. Again he was the only one who caught the apple, and he did not linger an instant but galloped off with it. The king grew angry and said, "That is not allowed; he must appear before me and tell his name." He gave the order that if the knight who caught the apple should go away again, they should pursue him, and if he would not come back willingly, they were to cut him down and stab him.

On the third day, the youth received from Iron John a suit of black armor and a black horse, and again he caught the apple. But when he was riding off with it, the king's attendants pursued him, and one of them got so near him that he wounded the youth's leg with the point of his sword. The youth nevertheless escaped from them, but his horse leapt so violently that the helmet fell from the youth's head, and they could see that he had golden hair. They rode back and announced this to the king.

The following day, the king's daughter asked the gardener about his boy. "He is at work in the garden; the odd creature has been at the festival, too, and only came home yesterday evening; he has likewise shown my children three golden apples that he has won."

The king had the boy summoned into his presence, and he came and again had his little cap on his head. But the king's daughter went up to him and took it off, and then his golden hair fell down over his shoulders, and he was so handsome that all were amazed. "Art thou the knight who came every day to the festival, always in different colors, and who caught the three golden apples?" asked the king.

"Yes," answered he, "and here the apples are," and he took them out of his pocket and returned them to the king. "If you desire further proof, you may see the wound that your people gave me when they followed me. But I am likewise the knight who helped you to your victory over your enemies."

"If thou canst perform such deeds as that, thou art

no gardener's boy; tell me, who is thy father?"

"My father is a mighty king, and gold have I in plenty as great as I require."

"I well see," said the king, "that I owe thanks to thee; can I do anything to please thee?"

"Yes," answered he, "that indeed you can. Give me your daughter to wife."

The maiden laughed, and said, "He does not stand much on ceremony, but I have already seen by his golden hair that he was no gardener's boy." Then she went and kissed him.

His father and mother came to the wedding and were in great delight, for they had given up all hope of ever seeing their dear son again. And as they were sitting at the marriage feast, the music suddenly stopped, the doors opened, and a stately king came in with a great procession. He went up to the youth, embraced him, and said, "I am Iron John and was by enchantment a wild man, but thou hast set me free; all the treasures that I possess shall be thy property."

The Fisherman
and His Wife

THERE WAS ONCE UPON A TIME a fisherman, who lived with his wife in a miserable hovel close by the sea, and every day he went out fishing. Once as he was sitting with his rod, looking at the clear water, his line suddenly went down, far down below, and when he drew it up again he brought out a large flounder. Then the flounder said to him, "Hark, fisherman, I pray you, let me live; I am no flounder really, but an enchanted prince. What good will it do you to kill me? I should not be good to eat. Put me in the water again, and let me go."

"Come," said the fisherman, "there is no need for so many words about it—a fish that can talk I should certainly let go, anyhow." With that he put him back again into the clear water, and the flounder went to the bottom, leaving a long streak of blood behind him. Then the fisherman got up and went home to his wife in the hovel.

"Husband," said the woman, "have you caught nothing today?"

"No," said the man. "I did catch a flounder, who said

he was an enchanted prince, so I let him go again."

"Did you not wish for anything first?" said the woman.

"No," said the man. "What should I wish for?"

"Ah," said the woman, "it is surely hard to have to live always in this dirty hovel; you might have wished for a small cottage for us. Go back and call to him. Tell him we want to have a small cottage; he will certainly give us that."

"Ah," said the man, "why should I go there again?"

"Why?" said the woman. "You did catch him, and you let him go again; he is sure to do it. Go at once." The man still did not quite want to go but did not like to oppose his wife, so he went to the sea.

When he got there the sea was all green and yellow and no longer so smooth, so he stood still and said,

> "Flounder, flounder in the sea,
> Come, I pray thee, here to me;
> For my wife, good Ilsabil,
> Wills not as I would have her will."

Then the flounder came swimming to him and said, "Well what does she want, then?"

"Ah," said the man, "I did catch you, and my wife says I really ought to have wished for something. She does not like to live in a wretched hovel any longer. She would like to have a cottage."

"Go, then," said the flounder, "she has it already."

When the man went home, his wife was no longer in the hovel, but instead of it there stood a small cottage, and she was sitting on a bench before the door. Then she took him by the hand and said, "Just come inside, look, now isn't this a great deal better?" So they went in, and there was a small porch, and a pretty little parlor and bedroom, and a kitchen and pantry with the best of furniture, fitted up with the most beautiful things made of tin and brass, whatsoever was wanted. Behind the cottage there was a small yard with hens and ducks, and a little garden with flowers and fruit. "Look," said the wife, "is not that nice!"

"Yes," said the husband, "and so we must always think it—now we will live quite contented."

"We will think about that," said the wife. With that, they ate something and went to bed.

Everything went well for a week or a fortnight, and then the woman said, "Hark you, husband, this cottage is far too small for us, and the garden and yard are little; the flounder might just as well have given us a larger house. I should like to live in a great stone castle; go to the flounder and tell him to give us a castle."

"Ah, wife," said the man, "the cottage is quite good enough; why should we live in a castle?"

"What!" said the woman. "Just go there; the flounder can always do that."

"No, wife," said the man, "the flounder has just given us the cottage. I do not like to go back so soon; it might make him angry."

"Go," said the woman. "He can do it quite easily, and will be glad to do it; just you go to him."

The man's heart grew heavy, and he would not go. He said to himself, *It is not right*, and yet he went. When he came to the sea the water was quite purple and dark blue, and gray and thick, and no longer so green and yellow, but it was still quiet. And he stood there and said,

> "Flounder, flounder in the sea,
> Come, I pray thee, here to me;
> For my wife, good Ilsabil,
> Wills not as I would have her will."

"Well, what does she want, then?" said the flounder.

"Alas," said the man, half scared, "she wants to live in a great stone castle."

"Go to it, then; she is standing before the door," said the flounder.

Then the man went away, intending to go home, but when he got there, he found a great stone palace. His wife was just standing on the steps going in, and she took him by the hand and said, "Come in." So he went in with her, and in the castle was a great hall paved with marble and many servants, who flung wide the doors.

The walls were all bright with beautiful hangings, and in the rooms were chairs and tables of pure gold, and crystal chandeliers hung from the ceiling, and all the rooms and bedrooms had carpets, and food and wine of the very best were standing on all the tables, so that they nearly broke down beneath it. Behind the house, too, there was a great courtyard, with stables for horses and cows, and the very best of carriages; there was a magnificent large garden, too, with the most beautiful flowers and fruit trees, and a park half a mile long, in which there were stags, deer, and hares, and everything that could be desired. "Come," said the woman, "isn't that beautiful?"

"Yes, indeed," said the man. "Now let it be; and we will live in this beautiful castle and be content."

"We will consider about that," said the woman, "and sleep upon it." Thereupon they went to bed.

The next morning the wife awoke first. It was just daybreak, and from her bed she saw the beautiful country lying before her. Her husband was still stretching himself, so she poked him in the side with her elbow and said, "Get up, husband, and just peep out of the window. Look you, couldn't we be the king over all that land? Go to the flounder; we will be the king."

"Ah, wife," said the man, "why should we be king? I do not want to be king."

"Well," said the wife, "if you won't be king, I will. Go to the flounder, for I will be king."

"Ah, wife," said the man, "why do you want to be king? I do not like to say that to him."

"Why not?" said the woman. "Go to him this instant; I must be king!"

So the man went and was quite unhappy because his wife wished to be king. *It is not right; it is not right,* thought he. He did not wish to go, but yet he went.

When he came to the sea, it was quite dark gray, and the water heaved up from below and smelt putrid. Then he went and stood by it, and said,

> "Flounder, flounder in the sea,
> Come, I pray thee, here to me;
> For my wife, good Ilsabil,
> Wills not as I would have her will."

"Well, what does she want, then?" said the flounder.

"Alas," said the man, "she wants to be king."

"Go to her; she is king already."

So the man went, and when he came to the palace, the castle had become much larger. It had a great tower and magnificent ornaments, the sentinel was standing before the door, and there were numbers of soldiers with kettle drums and trumpets. When he went inside the house, everything was of real marble and gold, with velvet covers and great golden tassels. Then the doors of the hall were opened, and there was the court in all its splendor; his wife was sitting on a high throne of gold and diamonds, with a great crown of gold on her head, and a scepter of pure gold and jewels in her hand. On both sides of her stood her maids-in-waiting in a row, each of them always one head shorter than the last.

Then he went and stood before her, and said, "Ah, wife, and now you are king."

"Yes," said the woman, "now I am king."

So he stood and looked at her, and when he had looked at her thus for some time, he said, "And now that you are king, let all else be, now we will wish for nothing more."

"Nay, husband," said the woman, quite anxiously, "I find time passes very heavily. I can bear it no longer; go to the flounder—I am king, but I must be emperor, too."

"Alas, wife, why do you wish to be emperor?"

"Husband," said she, "go to the flounder. I will be emperor."

"Alas, wife," said the man, "he cannot make you emperor; I may not say that to the fish. There is only one emperor in the land. An emperor the flounder cannot make you! I assure you he cannot."

"What!" said the woman. "I am the king, and you are nothing but my husband; will you go this moment? Go at once! If he can make a king, he can make an emperor. I will be emperor; go instantly."

So he was forced to go. As the man went, however, he was troubled in mind, and thought to himself, *It will not end well; it will not end well! Emperor is too shameless! The flounder will at last be tired out.*

With that he reached the sea, and the sea was quite black and thick. It began to boil up from below so that it threw up bubbles and such a sharp wind blew over it that it curdled, and the man was afraid. Then he went and stood by it and said,

> "Flounder, flounder in the sea,
> Come, I pray thee, here to me;
> For my wife, good Ilsabil,
> Wills not as I would have her will."

"Well, what does she want, then?" said the flounder.

"Alas, flounder," said he, "my wife wants to be emperor."

"Go to her," said the flounder. "She is emperor already."

So the man went, and when he got there the whole palace was made of polished marble with alabaster figures and golden ornaments, and soldiers were marching before the door blowing trumpets, and beating cymbals and drums. In the house, barons, counts, and dukes were going about as servants. Then they opened the doors to him, which were of pure gold. And when he entered, there sat his wife on a throne that was made of one piece of gold and was two miles high. She wore a great golden crown that was three yards high, set with diamonds and rubies; in one hand she had the scepter, and in the other the imperial orb. On both sides of her stood the yeomen of the guard in two rows, each being smaller than the one before him, from the biggest giant, who was two miles high, to the very smallest dwarf, just as big as my little finger. And before the throne stood a number of princes and dukes.

Then the man went and stood among them, and said, "Wife, are you emperor now?"

"Yes," said she, "now I am emperor."

Then he stood and looked at her well, and when he had looked at her thus for some time, he said, "Ah, wife, be content, now that you are emperor."

"Husband," said she, "why are you standing there? Now I am emperor, but I will be pope, too; go to the flounder."

"Alas, wife," said the man, "what will you not wish for? You cannot be pope. There is but one in Christendom. He cannot make you pope."

"Husband," said she, "I will be pope, go immediately, I must be pope this very day."

"No, wife," said the man, "I do not like to say that to him; that would not do, it is too much; the flounder can't make you pope."

"Husband," said she, "what nonsense! If he can make an emperor, he can make a pope. Go to him directly. I am emperor, and you are nothing but my husband; will you go at once?"

Then he was afraid and went; but he was quite faint, and shivered and shook, and his knees and legs trembled. A high wind blew over the land, the clouds flew, and toward evening all grew dark. The leaves fell from the trees, and the water rose and roared as if it were boiling, and splashed upon the shore. In the distance he saw ships that were firing guns in their sore need, pitching and tossing on the waves. And yet in the midst of the sky there was still a small bit of blue, though on every side it was as red as in a heavy storm. So, full of despair, he went and stood in much fear and said,

"Flounder, flounder in the sea,
Come, I pray thee, here to me;"
For my wife, good Ilsabil,
Wills not as I would have her will."

"Well, what does she want, then?" said the flounder.

"Alas," said the man, "she wants to be pope."

"Go to her, then," said the flounder. "She is pope already."

So he went, and when he got there, he saw what seemed to be a large church surrounded by palaces. He pushed his way through the crowd. Inside, however, everything was lighted up with thousands and thousands of candles. His wife was clad in gold and she was sitting on a much higher throne and she had three great golden crowns on. Around her there was much ecclesiastical splendor; on both sides of her was a row of candles, the largest of which was as tall as the very tallest tower, down to the very smallest kitchen candle. All the emperors and kings were on their knees before her, kissing her shoe.

"Wife," said the man, and looked attentively at her, "are you now pope?"

"Yes," said she, "I am pope."

So he stood and looked at her, and it was just as if he were looking at the bright sun. When he had stood looking at her thus for a short time, he said, "Ah, wife, if you are pope, do let well alone!" But she looked as stiff as a post and did not move or show any signs of life. Then said he, "Wife, now that you are pope, be satisfied; you cannot become anything greater now."

"I will consider about that," said the woman. Thereupon they both went to bed, but she was not satisfied, and greediness let her have no sleep, for she was continually thinking what there was left for her to be.

The man slept well and soundly, for he had run about a great deal during the day; but the woman could not fall asleep at all. She flung herself from one side to the other the whole night through, thinking always what more was left for her to be, but unable to call to mind anything else. At length the sun began to rise, and when the woman saw the red of dawn, she sat up in bed and looked at it. When, through the window, she saw the sun thus rising, she said, "Cannot I, too, order the sun and moon to rise?"

"Husband," she said, poking him in the ribs with her elbows, "wake up! Go to the flounder, for I wish to be even as God is."

The man was still half asleep, but he was so horrified that he fell out of bed. He thought he must have heard amiss; he rubbed his eyes and said, "Alas, wife, what are you saying?"

"Husband," said she, "if I can't order the sun and moon to rise, and have to look on and see the sun and moon rising, I can't bear it. I shall not know what it is to have another happy hour, unless I can make them rise myself." Then she looked at him so terribly that a shudder ran over him, and she said, "Go at once; I wish to be like unto God."

"Alas, wife," said the man, falling on his knees before her, "the flounder cannot do that; he can make an emperor and a pope; I beseech you, go on as you are, and be pope."

Then she fell into a rage, and her hair flew wildly

about her head, and she cried, "I will not endure this, I'll not bear it any longer; wilt thou go?" Then he put on his trousers and ran away like a madman. But outside a great storm was raging, and blowing so hard that he could scarcely keep his feet; houses and trees toppled over, the mountains trembled, rocks rolled into the sea, the sky was pitch-black, and it thundered and lightened, and the sea came in with black waves as high as church towers and mountains, and all with crests of white foam at the top. Then he cried, but could not hear his own words,

> "Flounder, flounder in the sea,
> Come, I pray thee, here to me;
> For my wife, good Ilsabil,
> Wills not as I would have her will."

"Well, what does she want, then?" said the flounder.

"Alas," said he, "she wants to be like unto God."

"Go to her, and you will find her back again in the dirty hovel."

And there they are living still at this very time.

Snow White and the Seven Dwarfs

ONCE UPON A TIME IN the middle of winter, when the flakes of snow were falling like feathers from the sky, a queen sat at a window sewing, and the frame of the window was made of black ebony. While she was sewing and looking out of the window at the snow, she pricked her finger with the needle, and three drops of blood fell upon the snow. The red looked pretty upon the white snow, and she thought to herself, *Would that I had a child as white as snow, as red as blood, and as black as the wood of the window frame.*

Soon after that she had a little daughter who was as white as snow, as red as blood, and whose hair was as black as ebony. She was therefore called little Snow White. And when the child was born, the queen died.

After a year had passed, the king took to himself another wife. She was a beautiful woman, but proud and haughty, and she could not bear that anyone else should surpass her in beauty. She had a wonderful looking glass, and when she stood in front of it and looked at herself in it, and said,

"Looking glass, looking glass, on the wall,
Who in this land is the fairest of all?"

The looking glass answered,

"Thou, O Queen, art the fairest of all!"

Then she was satisfied, for she knew that the looking glass spoke the truth.

But Snow White was growing up, and she grew more and more beautiful. When she was seven years old she was as beautiful as the day and more beautiful than the queen herself. Until one day, the queen asked her looking glass,

"Looking glass, looking glass, on the wall,
Who in this land is the fairest of all?"

Then, it answered,

"Thou art fairer, Lady Queen, than all within sight.
But more beautiful still, I believe, is Snow White."

Then the queen was shocked and turned yellow and green with envy. From that hour, whenever she looked at Snow White, her heart heaved in her breast, she hated the girl so much. Envy and pride grew higher and higher in her heart like a weed so that she had no peace day or night. She called a huntsman and said, "Take the child away into the forest; I will no longer have her in my sight. Kill her, and bring me back her heart as a token."

The huntsman obeyed and took her away. But when he had drawn his knife and was about to pierce Snow White's innocent heart, she began to weep and said, "Ah, dear huntsman, leave me my life! I will run away into the wild forest, and never come home again."

As she was so beautiful, the huntsman had pity on her and said, "Run away, then, you poor child." *The wild beasts will soon have devoured you*, thought he, and yet it seemed as if a stone had been rolled from his heart, since it was no longer needful for him to kill her. As a young boar just then came running by, he stabbed it, cut out its heart, and took it to the queen as proof that the child was dead. The cook had to salt this, and the wicked queen ate it and thought she had eaten the heart of Snow White.

But now the poor child was all alone in the great forest and so terrified that she looked at every leaf of every tree and did not know what to do. Then she began to run and ran over sharp stones and through thorns. The wild beasts ran past her but did her no harm.

She ran as long as her feet would go until it was almost evening; then she saw a little cottage and went into it to rest herself. Everything in the cottage was small but neater and cleaner than can be told. There was a table on which was a white cover and seven little plates, and on each plate a little spoon; moreover, there were seven little knives and forks, and seven little mugs. Against the wall stood seven little beds side by side, covered with snow-white counterpanes.

Little Snow White was so hungry and thirsty that she ate some vegetables and bread from each plate and drank a drop of wine out of each mug, for she did not wish to take all from one only. Then, as she was so tired, she laid herself down on one of the little beds, but none of them suited her; one was too long, another too short, but at last she found that the seventh one was right, and so she remained in it, said a prayer, and went to sleep.

When it was quite dark, the owners of the cottage came back; they were seven dwarfs who dug and delved in the mountains for ore. They lit their seven candles, and as it was now light within the cottage they saw that someone had been there, for everything was not in the same order in which they had left it.

The first said, "Who has been sitting on my chair?"

The second, "Who has been eating off my plate?"

The third, "Who has been taking some of my bread?"

The fourth, "Who has been eating my vegetables?"

The fifth, "Who has been using my fork?"

The sixth, "Who has been cutting with my knife?"

The seventh, "Who has been drinking out of my mug?"

Then the first looked around and saw that there was a little hole on his bed, and he said, "Who has been getting into my bed?"

The others came up and each called out, "Somebody has been lying in my bed, too." But the seventh when he looked at his bed saw little Snow White, who was lying asleep therein. He called the others, who came running up. They cried out with astonishment, brought their seven little candles, and let the light fall on little Snow White. "Oh, heavens! Oh, heavens!" cried they. "What a lovely child!" and they were so glad that they did not wake her up, but let her sleep on in the bed. And the seventh dwarf slept with his companions, one hour with each, and so got through the night.

When it was morning, little Snow White awoke and was frightened when she saw the seven dwarfs. But they were friendly and asked her what her name was.

"My name is Snow White," she answered.

"How have you come to our house?" said the dwarfs. Then she told them that her stepmother had wished to have her killed, but that the huntsman had spared her life, and that she had run for the whole day, until at last she had found their dwelling.

The dwarfs said, "If you will take care of our house, cook, make the beds, wash, sew, and knit, and if you will keep everything neat and clean, you can stay with us and you shall want for nothing."

"Yes," said Snow White, "with all my heart," and she stayed with them. She kept the house in order for them. In the mornings they went to the mountains and looked for copper and gold, and in the evenings they came back, and then their supper had to be ready.

The girl was alone the whole day, so the good dwarfs warned her and said, "Beware of your stepmother, she will soon know that you are here; be sure to let no one come in."

But the queen, believing that she had eaten Snow White's heart, could not but think that she was again the first and most beautiful of all. She went to her looking glass and said,

> "Looking glass, Looking glass, on the wall,
> Who in this land is the fairest of all?"

The glass answered,

> "O Queen, thou art fairest of all I see,
> But over the hills, where the seven dwarfs dwell,
> Snow White is still alive and well,
> And none is so fair as she."

Then she was astounded, for she knew that the looking glass never lied, and she knew that the huntsman had betrayed her, and that little Snow White was still alive. So she thought and thought again how she might kill her, for so long as she was not the fairest in the whole land, envy let her have no rest. When she had at last thought of something to do, she painted her face and dressed herself like an old peddler woman, and no one could have known her. In this disguise she went over the seven mountains to the seven dwarfs, knocked at the door, and cried, "Pretty things to sell, very cheap, very cheap."

Little Snow White looked out of the window and called out, "Good day, my good woman, what have you to sell?"

"Good things, pretty things," she answered, "corset laces of all colors," and she pulled out one that was woven of bright-colored silk.

I may let the worthy old woman in, thought Snow White, and she unbolted the door and bought the pretty laces.

"Child," said the old woman, "what a fright you look; come, I will lace you properly for once." Snow White had no suspicion but stood before her and let herself be laced with the new laces. But the old woman laced so quickly and so tightly that Snow White lost her breath and fell down as if dead. "Now I am the most beautiful," said the queen to herself, and ran away.

Not long afterward, in the evening, the seven dwarfs came home, but how shocked they were when they saw their dear little Snow White lying on the ground, and that she neither stirred nor moved, and seemed to be dead. They lifted her up, and, as they saw that she was laced too tightly, they cut the laces; then she began to breathe a little, and after a while came to life again. When the dwarfs heard what had happened, they said, "The old peddler woman was no one else than the wicked queen; take care and let no one come in when we are not with you."

But the wicked woman, when she had reached home, went in front of the glass and asked,

"Looking glass, Looking glass, on the wall,
Who in this land is the fairest of all?"

It answered as before,

"O Queen, thou art fairest of all I see,
But over the hills, where the seven dwarfs dwell,
Snow White is still alive and well,
And none is so fair as she."

When she heard that, all her blood rushed to her heart with fear, for she saw plainly that little Snow White was again alive. "But now," she said, "I will think of something that shall put an end to you," and by the help of witchcraft, which she understood, she made a poisonous comb. Then she disguised herself and took the shape of another old woman. So she went over the seven mountains to the seven dwarfs, knocked at the door, and cried, "Good things to sell, cheap, cheap!"

Little Snow White looked out and said, "Go away; I cannot let anyone come in."

"I suppose you can look," said the old woman, and she pulled the poisonous comb out and held it up. It pleased the girl so well that she let herself be beguiled and opened the door.

When they had made a bargain, the old woman said, "Now I will comb you properly for once." Poor little Snow White had no suspicion and let the old woman do as she pleased, but hardly had she put the comb in her hair than the poison in it took effect, and the girl fell down senseless. "You paragon of beauty," said the wicked woman, "you are done for now," and she went away.

But fortunately it was almost evening when the seven dwarfs came home. When they saw Snow White lying as if dead upon the ground they at once suspected the stepmother, and they looked and found the poisoned comb. Scarcely had they taken it out when Snow White came to herself and told them what had happened. Then they warned her once more to be upon her guard and to open the door to no one.

The queen, at home, went in front of the glass and said,

"Looking glass, Looking glass, on the wall,
Who in this land is the fairest of all?"

Then it answered as before,

"O Queen, thou art fairest of all I see,
But over the hills, where the seven dwarfs dwell,
Snow White is still alive and well,
And none is so fair as she."

When she heard the glass speak thus, she trembled and shook with rage. "Snow White shall die," she cried, "even if it costs me my life!"

Thereupon she went into a quite secret, lonely room, where no one ever came, and there she made a very poisonous apple. Outside it looked pretty, white with a red cheek so that everyone who saw it longed for it, but whoever ate a piece of it must surely die.

When the apple was ready she painted her face and dressed herself up as a country woman, and so she went over the seven mountains to the seven dwarfs. She knocked at the door. Snow White put her head out of the window and said, "I cannot let anyone in; the seven dwarfs have forbidden me."

"It is all the same to me," answered the woman. "I shall soon get rid of my apples. There, I will give you one."

"No," said Snow White, "I dare not take anything."

"Are you afraid of poison?" said the old woman. "Look, I will cut the apple in two pieces; you eat the red cheek, and I will eat the white." The apple was so cunningly made that only the red cheek was poisoned. Snow White longed for the fine apple, and when she saw that the woman ate part of it she could resist no longer and stretched out her hand and took the poisonous half. But hardly had she a bit of it in her mouth than she fell down dead. Then the queen looked at her with a dreadful look, laughed aloud, and said, "White as snow, red as blood, black as ebony wood! This time the dwarfs cannot wake you up again."

Then she asked of the looking glass at home,

"Looking glass, looking glass, on the wall,
Who in this land is the fairest of all?"

It answered at last,

"O Queen, in this land thou art fairest of all."

Then her envious heart had rest, so far as an envious heart can have rest.

The dwarfs, when they came home in the evening, found Snow White lying upon the ground; she breathed no longer and was dead. They lifted her up, looked to see whether they could find anything poisonous, unlaced her, combed her hair, and washed her with water and wine, but it was all of no use; the poor child was dead, and remained dead. They laid her upon a bier, and all seven of them sat around it and wept for her, and wept three days long.

Then they were going to bury her, but she still looked as if she were living and still had her pretty red cheeks. They said, "We could not bury her in the dark ground," and they had a transparent coffin of glass made so that she could be seen from all sides. They laid her in it and wrote her name upon it in golden letters and wrote that she was a king's daughter. Then they put the coffin out upon the mountain, and one of them always stayed by it and watched it. Birds came, too, and wept for Snow White; first an owl, then a raven, and last a dove.

And now Snow White lay a long, long time in the coffin, and she did not change but looked as if she were asleep; for she was as white as snow, as red as blood, and her hair was as black as ebony.

It happened, however, that a king's son came into the forest and went to the dwarfs' house to spend the night. He saw the coffin on the mountain, and the beautiful Snow White within it, and he read what was written upon it in golden letters. Then he said to the dwarfs, "Let me have the coffin; I will give you whatever you want for it."

But the dwarfs answered, "We will not part with it for all the gold in the world."

Then he said, "Let me have it as a gift, for I cannot live without seeing Snow White. I will honor and prize her as my dearest possession." As he spoke in this way, the good dwarfs took pity upon him and gave him the coffin.

And now the king's son had it carried away by his servants on their shoulders. And it happened that they stumbled over a tree stump, and with the shock, the poisonous piece of apple that Snow White had bitten off came out of her throat. Before long she opened her eyes, lifted up the lid of the coffin, sat up, and was once more alive. "Oh, heavens, where am I?" she cried.

The king's son, full of joy, said, "You are with me," told her what had happened, and said, "I love you more than everything in the world; come with me to my father's palace, you shall be my wife."

Snow White was willing, and went with him, and their wedding was held with great show and splendor. But Snow White's wicked stepmother was also bidden to the feast. When she had arrayed herself in beautiful clothes she went before the looking glass and said,

> "Looking glass, looking glass, on the wall,
> Who in this land is the fairest of all?"

The glass answered,

> "O Queen, of all here the fairest art thou,
> But the young queen is fairer by far even now."

Then the wicked woman uttered a curse, and was so

wretched, so utterly wretched, that she knew not what to do. At first she would not go to the wedding at all, but she had no peace and must go to see the young queen. When she went in she knew Snow White; she stood still with rage and fear, and could not stir. But the dwarfs had forged iron slippers and set them upon the fire; they brought them in with tongs and set them before her. Then they forced her to put on the red-hot shoes and dance until she dropped down dead.

Cat and Mouse in Partnership

A CERTAIN CAT HAD MADE the acquaintance of a mouse, and had said so much to her about the great love and friendship she felt for her, that at length the mouse agreed that they should live and keep house together. "But we must make a provision for winter, or else we shall suffer from hunger," said the cat, "and you, little mouse, cannot venture everywhere, or you will be caught in a trap someday."

The good advice was followed, and a pot of fat was bought, but they did not know where to put it. At length, after much consideration, the cat said, "I know no place where it will be better stored up than in the church, for no one dares take anything away from there. We will set it beneath the altar and not touch it until we are really in need of it." So the pot was placed in safety, but it was not long before the cat had a great yearning for it, and said to the mouse, "I want to tell you something, little mouse; my cousin has brought a little son into the world and has asked me to be godmother; he is white with brown spots, and I am to hold him over the font at the christening. Let me go out today, and you look after the house by yourself."

"Yes, yes," answered the mouse, "by all means go, and if you get anything very good, think of me. I should like a drop of sweet red christening wine, too."

All this, however, was untrue; the cat had no cousin, and had not been asked to be godmother. She went straight to the church, stole to the pot of fat, began to lick at it, and licked the top of the fat off. Then she took a walk upon the roofs of the town, looked out for opportunities, and then stretched herself in the sun, licked her lips whenever she thought of the pot of fat, and not until it was evening did she return home. "Well, here you are again," said the mouse, "no doubt you have had a merry day."

"All went off well," answered the cat.

"What name did they give the child?"

"Top-off!" said the cat quite coolly.

"Top-off!" cried the mouse. "That is a very odd and uncommon name; is it a usual one in your family?"

"What it signifies," said the cat, "is no worse than Crumb-stealer, as your godchildren are called."

Before long, the cat was seized by another fit of longing. She said to the mouse, "You must do me a favor, and once more manage the house for a day alone. I am again asked to be godmother, and, as the child has a white ring round its neck, I cannot refuse." The good mouse consented, but the cat crept behind the town walls to the church and devoured half the pot of fat. "Nothing ever seems so good as what one keeps to oneself," said she, and was quite satisfied with her day's work.

When she went home the mouse inquired, "And what was this child christened?"

"Half-done," answered the cat.

"Half-done! What are you saying? I never heard the name in my life; I'll wager anything it is not in the calendar!"

The cat's mouth soon began to water for some more licking. "All good things go in threes," said she. "I am asked to stand godmother again. The child is quite black, only it has white paws. But with that exception, it has not a single white hair on its whole body; this only happens once every few years, you will let me go, won't you?"

"Top-off! Half-done!" answered the mouse. "They are such odd names, they make me very thoughtful."

"You sit at home," said the cat, "in your dark gray fur coat and long tail, and are filled with fancies; that's because you do not go out in the daytime."

During the cat's absence the mouse cleaned the house and put it in order, but the greedy cat entirely emptied the pot of fat. *When everything is eaten up, one has some peace*, said she to herself. Well filled and fat, she did not return home till night. The mouse at once asked what name had been given to the third child. "It will not please you more than the others," said the cat. "He is called All-gone."

"All-gone," cried the mouse, "that is the most suspicious name of all! I have never seen it in print. All-gone; what can that mean?" and she shook her head, curled herself up, and lay down to sleep.

From this time forth, no one invited the cat to be godmother, but when the winter had come and there was no longer anything to be found outside, the mouse thought of their provision and said, "Come, cat, we will go to our pot of fat that we have stored up for ourselves—we shall enjoy that."

"Yes," answered the cat, "you will enjoy it as much as you would enjoy sticking that dainty tongue of yours out of the window."

They set out on their way, but when they arrived, the pot of fat certainly was still in its place, but it was empty. "Alas!" said the mouse. "Now I see what has happened; now it comes to light! You are a true fiend! You have devoured all when you were standing godmother. First top off, then half done, then—"

"Will you hold your tongue?" cried the cat. "One word more and I will eat you, too."

"All gone" was already on the poor mouse's lips; scarcely had she spoken it before the cat sprang on her, seized her, and swallowed her down. Verily, that is the way of the world.

The Golden Bird

IN THE OLDEN TIME THERE was a king, who had behind his palace a beautiful pleasure-garden in which there was a tree that bore golden apples. When the apples were getting ripe they were counted, but on the very next morning one was missing. This was told to the king, and he ordered that a watch should be kept every night beneath the tree.

The king had three sons, the eldest of whom he sent, as soon as night came on, into the garden; but when midnight came he could not keep himself from sleeping, and next morning again an apple was gone.

The following night the second son had to keep watch, and it fared no better with him. As soon as twelve o'clock had struck he fell asleep, and in the morning an apple was gone.

Now it came to the turn of the third son to watch; he was quite ready, but the king had not much trust in him, and thought that he would be of less use even than his brothers, but at last he let him go. The youth lay down beneath the tree, but kept awake, and did not let sleep master him. When it struck twelve, something rustled through the air, and in the moonlight he saw a bird coming whose feathers were all shining with gold. The bird alighted on the tree and had just plucked off an apple, when the youth shot an arrow at him. The bird flew off, but the arrow had struck his plumage, and one of his golden feathers fell down. The youth picked it up, and the next morning took it to the king and told him what he had seen in the night. The king called his council together, and everyone declared that a feather like this was worth more than the whole kingdom. "If the feather is so precious," declared the king, "one alone will not do for me; I must and will have the whole bird!"

The eldest son set out. He thought that he would easily find the Golden Bird. When he had gone some distance he saw a fox sitting at the edge of a wood, so he cocked his gun and took aim at him. The fox cried, "Do not shoot me! In return I will give you some good counsel. You are on the way to the Golden Bird, and this evening you will come to a village in which stand two inns opposite to one another. One of them is lighted up brightly, and all goes on merrily within, but do not go into it; go rather into the other, even though it seems a bad one."

How can such a silly beast give wise advice? thought the king's son, and he pulled the trigger. But he missed the fox, who stretched out his tail and ran quickly into the woods.

So he pursued his way, and by evening came to the village where the two inns were; in one they were singing and dancing; the other had a poor, miserable look. *I should be a fool, indeed*, he thought, *if I were to go into the shabby tavern and pass by the good one*. So he went into the cheerful one, lived there in riot and revel, and forgot the bird and his father, and all good counsels.

When some time had passed, and the eldest son for month after month did not come back home, the second set out, wishing to find the Golden Bird. The fox met him as he had met the eldest and gave him the good advice, of which he took no heed. He came to the two inns and standing at the window of the one from which came the music was his brother, who called out to him. He could not resist, but went inside and lived only for pleasure.

Again some time passed, then the king's youngest son wanted to set off and try his luck, but his father would not allow it. "It is of no use," said he. "He will find the Golden Bird still less than his brothers, and if a mishap were to befall him, he knows not how to help himself; he is a little wanting at the best." But at last, as he had no peace, he let him go.

Again the fox was sitting outside the woods, and begged for his life and offered his good advice. The youth was good-natured and said, "Be easy, little fox, I will do you no harm."

"You shall not repent it," answered the fox. "And that you may get on more quickly, get up behind on my tail." Scarcely had he seated himself when the fox began to run, and away he went over stock and stone till his hair whistled in the wind. When they came to the village the youth got off; he followed the good advice, and without looking around turned into the little inn, where he spent the night quietly.

The next morning, as soon as he got into the open country, there sat the fox already, who said, "I will tell you further what you have to do. Go on quite straight, and at last you will come to a castle, in front of which a whole regiment of soldiers is lying, but do not trouble yourself about them, for they will all be asleep and snoring. Go through the midst of them straight into the castle, and go through all the rooms, till at last you will come to a chamber where a Golden Bird is hanging in a wooden cage. Close by, there stands an empty gold cage for show, but beware of taking the bird out of the common cage and putting it into the fine one, or it may go badly with you." With these words the fox again stretched out his tail, and the king's son seated himself upon it, and away he went over stock and stone till his hair whistled in the wind.

When he came to the castle he found everything as

the fox had said. The king's son went into the chamber where the Golden Bird was shut up in a wooden cage, while a golden one stood hard by; and the three golden apples lay about the room. *But*, thought he, *it would be absurd if I were to leave the beautiful bird in the common and ugly cage*, so he opened the door, laid hold of it, and put it into the golden cage. But at the same moment the bird uttered a shrill cry. The soldiers awoke, rushed in, and took him off to prison. The next morning he was taken before a court of justice, and since he confessed everything, was sentenced to death.

This king, however, said that he would grant him his life on one condition: namely, if he brought him the Golden Horse that ran faster than the wind. In that case he should receive, over and above, as a reward, the Golden Bird.

The prince set off, but he sighed and was sorrowful, for how was he to find the Golden Horse? But all at once he saw his old friend the fox sitting on the road. "Look you," said the fox, "this has happened because you did not give heed to me. However, be of good courage. I will give you my help and tell you how to get to the Golden Horse. You must go straight on, and you will come to a castle, where in the stable stands the horse. The grooms will be lying in front of the stable; but they will be asleep and snoring, and you can quietly lead out the Golden Horse. But of one thing you must take heed; put on him the common saddle of wood and leather, and not the golden one, which hangs close by, else it will go ill with you." Then the fox stretched out his tail, the prince seated himself upon it, and away he went over stock and stone until his hair whistled in the wind.

Everything happened just as the fox had said; the prince came to the stable in which the Golden Horse was standing, but just as he was going to put the common saddle upon him, he thought, *It will be a shame to such a beautiful beast if I do not give him the good saddle, which belongs to him by right.* But scarcely had the golden saddle touched the horse than he began to neigh loudly. The grooms awoke, seized the youth, and threw him into prison. The next morning he was sentenced by the court to death; but their king promised to grant him his life, and the Golden Horse as well, if he could bring back the beautiful princess from the Golden Castle.

With a heavy heart the youth set out; yet luckily for him he soon found the trusty fox. "I ought only to leave you to your ill luck," said the fox, "but I pity you and will help you once more out of your trouble. This road takes you straight to the Golden Castle. You will reach it by eventide, and at night·when everything is quiet, the beautiful princess goes to the bathing house to bathe. When she enters it, run up to her and give her a kiss; then she will follow you, and you can take her away with you. Only, do not allow her to take leave of her parents first, or it will go ill with you."

Then the fox stretched out his tail, the king's son seated himself upon it, and away the fox went, over stock and stone, till his hair whistled in the wind.

When he reached the Golden Castle it was just as the fox had said. He waited until midnight, when everything lay in deep sleep, and the beautiful princess was going to the bathing house. Then he sprang out and gave her a kiss. She said that she would like to go with him, but she asked him pitifully, and with tears, to allow her first to take leave of her parents. At first he withstood her prayer, but when she wept more and more, and fell at his feet, he at last gave in. But no sooner had the maiden reached the bedside of her father than he and all the rest in the castle awoke, and the youth was laid hold of and put into prison.

The next morning the King of the Golden Castle said to him, "Your life is forfeited, and you can only find mercy if you take away the hill that stands in front of my windows and prevents my seeing beyond it. You must finish it all within eight days. If you do that, you shall have my daughter as your reward."

The prince began, and dug and shoveled without

leaving off, but when after seven days he saw how little he had done, and how all his work was as good as nothing, he fell into great sorrow and gave up all hope. But on the evening of the seventh day the fox appeared and said, "You do not deserve that I should take any trouble about you; but just go away and lie down to sleep, and I will do the work for you."

The next morning when he awoke and looked out of the window, the hill had gone. The youth ran, full of joy, to the king and told him that the task was fulfilled, and whether he liked it or not, the king had to hold to his word and give him his daughter.

So the two set forth together, and it was not long before the trusty fox came up with them. "You have certainly got what is best," said he, "but the Golden Horse also belongs to the Maiden of the Golden Castle."

"How shall I get it?" asked the youth.

"That I will tell you," answered the fox. "First take the beautiful maiden to the king who sent you to the Golden Castle. There will be unheard-of rejoicing; they will gladly give you the Golden Horse, and will bring it out to you. Mount it as soon as possible and offer your hand to all in farewell; last of all to the beautiful maiden. And as soon as you have taken her hand, swing her up onto the horse and gallop away, and no one will be able to bring you back, for the horse runs faster than the wind."

All was accomplished successfully, and the prince carried off the beautiful princess on the Golden Horse.

The fox did not remain behind, and he said to the youth, "Now I will help you to get the Golden Bird. When you come near to the castle where the Golden Bird is to be found, let the maiden get down, and I will take her into my care. Then ride with the Golden Horse into the castle yard; there will be great rejoicing at the sight, and they will bring out the Golden Bird for you. As soon as you have the cage in your hand, gallop back to us and take the maiden away again."

When the plan had succeeded, and the king's son was about to ride home with his treasures, the fox said, "Now you shall reward me for my help."

"What do you require for it?" asked the youth.

"When you get into the wood yonder, shoot me dead, and chop off my head and feet."

"That would be fine gratitude," said the king's son. "I cannot possibly do that for you."

The fox said, "If you will not do it, I must leave you, but before I go away I will give you a piece of good advice. Be careful about two things. Buy no gallows'-flesh, and do not sit at the edge of any well." And then he ran into the woods.

The youth thought, *That is a wonderful beast, he has strange whims; who is going to buy gallows'-flesh? And the desire to sit at the edge of a well has never yet seized me.*

He rode on with the beautiful maiden, and his road took him again through the village in which his two brothers had remained. There was a great stir and noise, and, when he asked what was going on, he was told that two men were going to be hanged. As he came nearer to the place he saw that they were his brothers, who had been playing all kinds of wicked pranks, and had squandered all their wealth. He inquired whether they could not be set free. "If you will pay for them," answered the people. "But why should you waste your money on wicked men, and buy them free?" He did not think twice about it, but paid for them, and when they were set free they all went on their way together.

They came to the woods where the fox had first met them. As it was cool and pleasant within it, the two elder brothers said, "Let us rest a little by the well, and eat and drink." The prince agreed, and while they were talking, he forgot himself and sat down upon the edge of the well without thinking of any evil. But the two brothers threw him backward into the well, took the maiden, the horse, and the bird, and went home to their father. "Here we bring you not only the Golden Bird," said they, "we have won the Golden Horse also, and the Maiden of the Golden Castle." Then was there great joy; but the horse would not eat, the bird would not sing, and the maiden sat and wept.

But the youngest brother was not dead. By good fortune the well was dry, and he fell upon soft moss without being hurt, but he could not get out again. Even in this strait the faithful fox did not leave him: He came and leapt down to him, and upbraided him for having forgotten his advice. "But yet I cannot give it up so," the fox said. "I will help you up again into day-light." He bade him grasp his tail and keep tight hold of it, and then he pulled him up.

"You are not out of all danger yet," said the fox. "Your brothers were not sure of your death and have surrounded the wood with watchers, who are to kill you if you let yourself be seen." But a poor man was sitting upon the road, with whom the youth changed clothes, and in this way he got to the king's palace.

No one knew him, but the bird began to sing, the horse began to eat, and the beautiful maiden left off weeping. The king, astonished, asked, "What does this mean?"

Then the maiden said, "I do not know, but I have been so sorrowful and now I am so happy! I feel as if my true bridegroom had come." She told him all that had happened, although the other brothers had threatened her with death if she were to betray anything.

The king commanded that all people who were in his castle should be brought before him. Among them came the youth in his ragged clothes, but the maiden knew him at once and fell upon his neck. The wicked brothers were seized and put to death, but he was married to the beautiful maiden and declared heir to the king.

But how did it fare with the poor fox? Long afterward, the king's son was once again walking in the wood, when the fox met him and said, "You have everything now that you can wish for, but there is never an end to my misery, and yet it is in your power to free me." Again he asked him with tears to shoot him dead and chop off his head and feet. So he did it, and scarcely was it done when the fox was changed into a man, and was no other than the brother of the beautiful princess, who at last was freed from the magic charm that had been laid upon him. And now nothing more was wanting to their happiness as long as they lived.

The Twelve Huntsmen

THERE WAS ONCE A KING'S son who was betrothed to a maiden whom he loved very much. When he was sitting beside her and very happy, news came that his father lay sick unto death and desired to see him once again before his end. Then the son said to his beloved, "I must now go and leave thee, I give thee a ring as a remembrance of me. When I am king, I will return and fetch thee."

So he rode away, and when he reached his father, the latter was dangerously ill and near his death. He said to him, "Dear son, I wished to see thee once again before my end; promise me to marry as I wish." Then he named a certain king's daughter who was to be his wife. The son was in such trouble that he did not think what he was doing, and said, "Yes, dear father, your will shall be done," and thereupon the king shut his eyes, and died.

When therefore the son had been proclaimed king, and the time of mourning was over, he was forced to keep the promise that he had given his father. He caused the other king's daughter to be asked in marriage, and she was promised to him. His first betrothed heard of this, and fretted so much about his faithlessness that she nearly died. Then her father said to her, "Dearest child, why art thou so sad? Thou shalt have whatsoever thou wilt."

She thought for a moment and said, "Dear father, I wish for eleven girls exactly like myself in face, figure, and size."

The father said, "If it be possible, thy desire shall be fulfilled," and he caused a search to be made in his whole kingdom, until eleven young maidens were found who exactly resembled his daughter in face, figure, and size.

When they came to the princess, she had twelve suits of huntsmen's clothes made, all alike. The eleven maidens had to put on the huntsmen's clothes, and she herself put on the twelfth suit. Thereupon she took leave of her father, rode away with them, and rode to the court of her former betrothed, whom she loved so dearly. Then she inquired if he required any huntsmen, and if he would take the whole of them into his service. The king looked at her and did not know her, but as they were such handsome fellows, he said yes, and that he would willingly take them, and now they were the king's twelve huntsmen.

The king, however, had a lion, which was a wondrous animal, for he knew all concealed and secret things. It came to pass that one evening the lion said to the king, "Thou thinkest thou hast twelve huntsmen?"

"Yes," said the king, "they are twelve huntsmen." The lion continued, "Thou art mistaken; they are twelve girls."

The king said, "That cannot be true! How wilt thou prove that to me?"

"Oh, just let some peas be strewn in thy antechamber," answered the lion, "and then thou wilt soon see it. Men have a firm step, and when they walk over the peas none of them stir, but girls trip and skip, and drag their feet, and the peas roll about." The king was well pleased with the counsel and caused the peas to be strewn.

There was, however, a servant of the king's who favored the huntsmen, and when he heard that they were going to be put to this test he went to them, repeated everything, and said, "The lion wants to make the king believe that you are girls."

Then the king's daughter thanked him and said to her maidens, "Put on some strength, and step firmly on the peas."

So next morning when the king had the twelve huntsmen called before him, and they came into the antechamber where the peas were lying, they stepped so firmly on them, and had such a strong, sure walk, that not one of the peas either rolled or stirred. Then they went away again, and the king said to the lion, "Thou hast lied to me; they walk just like men."

The lion said, "They have got to know that they were going to be put to the test and have assumed some strength. Just let twelve spinning wheels be brought into the antechamber someday, and they will go to them and be pleased with them, and that is what no man would do." The king liked the advice and had the spinning wheels placed in the antechamber.

But the servant, who was well disposed to the huntsmen, went to them and disclosed the project. Then when they were alone, the princess said to her eleven girls, "Put some constraint on yourselves, and do not look round at the spinning wheels." Next morning when the king had his twelve huntsmen summoned, they went through the antechamber, and never once looked at the spinning wheels.

Then the king again said to the lion, "Thou hast deceived me; they are men, for they have not looked at the spinning wheels."

The lion replied, "They have learnt that they were going to be put to the test, and have restrained themselves." The king, however, would no longer believe the lion.

The twelve huntsmen always followed the king to the chase, and his liking for them continually increased. Now it came to pass that once when they were out hunting, news came that the king's betrothed was approaching. When the true bride heard that, it hurt her so much that her heart was almost broken, and she fell fainting to the ground. The king thought something had happened to his dear huntsman, ran up to him, wanted to help him, and drew his glove off. Then he saw the ring that he had given to his first bride, and when he looked in her face he recognized her. Then his heart was so touched that he kissed her, and when she opened her eyes, he said, "Thou art mine, and I am thine, and no one in the world can alter that." He sent a messenger to the other bride, and entreated her to return to her own kingdom, for he had a wife already, and a man who had just found an old love did not require a new one. Thereupon the wedding was celebrated, and the lion was again taken into favor, because, after all, he had told the truth.

Cinderella

THE WIFE OF A RICH man fell sick, and as she felt that her end was drawing near, she called her only daughter to her bedside and said, "Dear child, be good and pious, and then the good God will always protect thee, and I will look down on thee from heaven and be near thee." Thereupon she closed her eyes and departed. Every day the maiden went out to her mother's grave and wept, and she remained pious and good. When winter came the snow spread a white sheet over the grave, and when the spring sun had drawn it off again, the man had taken another wife.

The woman had brought two daughters into the house with her, who were beautiful and fair of face, but vile and black of heart. Now began a bad time for the poor stepchild. "Is the stupid goose to sit in the parlor with us?" said they. "He who wants to eat bread must earn it; out with the kitchen wench." They took her pretty clothes away from her, put an old gray bedgown on her, and gave her wooden shoes. "Just look at the proud princess, how decked out she is!" they cried, and laughed, and they led her into the kitchen. There she had to do hard work from morning till night, get up before daybreak, carry water, light fires, cook, and wash. Besides this, the sisters did her every imaginable injury—they mocked her and emptied her peas and lentils into the ashes, so that she was forced to sit and pick them out again. In the evening when she had worked till she was weary, she had no bed to go to but had to sleep by the fireside in the ashes. And as on that account she always looked dusty and dirty, they called her Cinderella.

It happened that the father was once going to the fair, and he asked his two stepdaughters what he should bring back for them.

"Beautiful dresses," said one.

"Pearls and jewels," said the second.

"And thou, Cinderella," said he, "what wilt thou have?"

"Father, break off for me the first branch that knocks against your hat on your way home." So he bought beautiful dresses, pearls, and jewels for his two stepdaughters, and on his way home, as he was riding through a green thicket, a hazel twig brushed against him and knocked off his hat. Then he broke off the branch and took it with him. When he reached home he gave his stepdaughters the things they had wished for, and to Cinderella he gave the branch from the hazel bush. Cinderella thanked him, went to her mother's grave, planted the branch on it, and wept so much that the tears fell down on it and watered it. It grew and became a handsome tree. Thrice a day Cinderella went and sat beneath it, wept, and prayed, and a little white bird always came onto the tree, and if Cinderella expressed a wish, the bird threw down to her what she had wished for.

It happened, however, that the king appointed a festival that was to last three days, and to which all the beautiful young girls in the country were invited, in order that his son might choose himself a bride. When the two stepsisters heard that they, too, were to appear among the number, they were delighted. They called Cinderella and said, "Comb our hair for us, brush our shoes, and fasten our buckles, for we are going to the festival at the king's palace."

Cinderella obeyed, but wept, because she, too, would have liked to go with them to the dance, and she begged her stepmother to allow her to do so. "Thou go, Cinderella!" said she. "Thou art dusty and dirty and wouldst go to the festival? Thou hast no clothes and shoes, and yet wouldst dance!" As, however, Cinderella went on asking, the stepmother at last said, "I have emptied a dish of lentils into the ashes for thee, if thou hast picked them out again in two hours, thou shalt go with us."

The maiden went through the back door into the garden and called, "You tame pigeons, you turtledoves, and all you birds beneath the sky, come and help me to pick . . .

> "The good into the pot,
> The bad into the crop."

Then two white pigeons came in by the kitchen window, and afterward the turtledoves, and at last all the birds beneath the sky came whirring and crowding in, and alighted among the ashes. The pigeons nodded with their heads and began to pick, pick, pick, pick, and the rest began also to pick, pick, pick, pick, and gathered all the good grains into the dish. Hardly had one hour passed before they had finished, and all flew out again. Then the girl took the dish to her stepmother, and was glad, and believed that now she would be allowed to go with them to the festival.

But the stepmother said, "No, Cinderella, thou hast no clothes and thou canst not dance; thou wouldst only be laughed at." And as Cinderella wept at this, the stepmother said, "If thou canst pick two dishes of lentils out of the ashes for me in one hour, thou shalt go with us." And she thought to herself, *That she most certainly cannot do*. When the stepmother had emptied the two dishes of lentils among the ashes, the maiden went through the back door into the garden and cried, "You tame pigeons, you turtledoves, and all you birds under heaven, come and help me to pick . . .

> "The good into the pot,
> The bad into the crop."

Then two white pigeons came in by the kitchen window, and afterward the turtledoves, and at length all the birds beneath the sky came whirring and crowding in, and alighted among the ashes. The doves nodded with their heads and began to pick, pick, pick, pick, and the others began also to pick, pick, pick, pick, and gathered all the good seeds into the dishes, and before half an hour was over they had already finished, and all flew out again. Then the maiden carried the dishes to the stepmother and was delighted, and believed that she might now go with them to the festival. But the stepmother said, "All this will not help thee; thou goest not with us, for thou hast no clothes and canst not dance; we should be ashamed of thee!" On this she turned her back on Cinderella and hurried away with her two proud daughters.

As no one was now at home, Cinderella went to her mother's grave beneath the hazel tree and cried,

> "Shiver and quiver, little tree,
> Silver and gold throw down over me."

Then the bird threw a gold and silver dress down to

her, and slippers embroidered with silk and silver. She put on the dress with all speed and went to the festival. Her stepsisters and the stepmother, however, did not know her, and thought she must be a foreign princess, for she looked so beautiful in the golden dress. They never once thought of Cinderella, and believed that she was sitting at home in the dirt, picking lentils out of the ashes. The prince went to meet her, took her by the hand, and danced with her. He would dance with no other maiden and never left loose of her hand, and if anyone else came to invite her, he said, "This is my partner."

She danced till it was evening, and then she wanted to go home. But the king's son said, "I will go with thee and bear thee company," for he wished to see to whom the beautiful maiden belonged. She escaped from him, however, and sprang into the pigeon house.

The king's son waited until her father came, and then he told him that the stranger maiden had leapt into the pigeon house. The old man thought, *Can it be Cinderella?* and they had to bring him an axe and a pickaxe so that he might hew the pigeon house to pieces, but no one was inside it. When they got home, Cinderella lay in her dirty clothes among the ashes, and a dim little oil lamp was burning on the mantlepiece. Cinderella had jumped quickly down from the back of the pigeon house and had run to the little hazel tree, where she had taken off her beautiful clothes and laid them on the grave, and the bird had taken them away again, and then she had placed herself in the kitchen among the ashes in her gray gown.

Next day when the festival began afresh, and her parents and the stepsisters had gone once more, Cinderella went to the hazel tree and said,

"Shiver and quiver, my little tree,
Silver and gold throw down over me."

Then the bird threw down a much more beautiful dress than on the preceding day. When Cinderella appeared at the festival in this dress, everyone was astonished at her beauty. The king's son had waited until she came, and he instantly took her by the hand and danced with no one but her. When others came and invited her, he said, "She is my partner." When evening came she wished to leave, and the king's son followed her and wanted to see into which house she went. But she sprang away from him into the garden behind the house. Therein stood a beautiful tall tree, on which hung the most magnificent pears. She clambered so nimbly between the branches, like a squirrel, that the king's son did not know where she was gone. He waited until her father came, and said to him, "The stranger maiden has escaped from me, and I believe she has climbed up the pear tree."

The father thought, *Can it be Cinderella?* and had an axe brought and cut the tree down, but no one was on it. When they got into the kitchen, Cinderella lay there among the ashes, as usual, for she had jumped down on the other side of the tree, taken the beautiful dress to the bird on the little hazel tree, and put on her gray gown.

On the third day, when the parents and sisters had gone away, Cinderella went once more to her mother's grave and said to the little tree,

"Shiver and quiver, my little tree,
Silver and gold throw down over me."

Now the bird threw down to her a dress that was more splendid and magnificent than any she had yet had, and the slippers were golden. When she went to the festival in the dress, no one knew how to speak for astonishment. The king's son danced with her only, and if anyone invited her to dance, he said, "She is my partner."

When evening came, Cinderella wished to leave, and the king's son was anxious to go with her, but she escaped from him so quickly that he could not follow her. The king's son had, however, used a stratagem, and had caused the whole staircase to be smeared with pitch. There, when she ran down, the maiden's left slipper remained sticking. The king's son picked it up, and it was small and dainty and all golden. Next morning, he went with it to the father and said to him, "No one shall be my wife but she whose foot this golden slipper fits."

Then were the two sisters glad, for they had pretty feet. The eldest went with the shoe into her room and wanted to try it on, and her mother stood by. But she could not get her big toe into it; the shoe was too small for her. Then her mother gave her a knife and said, "Cut the toe off; when thou art queen, thou wilt have no more need to go on foot." The maiden cut the toe off, forced the foot into the shoe, swallowed the pain, and went out to the king's son. Then he took her on his horse as his bride and rode away with her. They were, however, obliged to pass the grave—and there on the hazel tree sat the two pigeons, who cried,

> "Turn and peep, turn and peep,
> There's blood within the shoe,
> The shoe it is too small for her,
> The true bride waits for you."

Then he looked at her foot and saw how the blood was streaming from it. He turned his horse around, took the false bride home again, and said she was not the true one, and that the other sister was to put the shoe on. Then this one went into her chamber and got her toes safely into the shoe, but her heel was too large.

So her mother gave her a knife and said, "Cut a bit off thy heel; when thou art queen, thou wilt have no more need to go on foot." The maiden cut a bit off her heel, forced her foot into the shoe, swallowed the pain, and went out to the king's son. He took her on his horse as his bride and rode away with her, but when they passed by the hazel tree, two little pigeons sat on it and cried,

> "Turn and peep, turn and peep,
> There's blood within the shoe
> The shoe it is too small for her,
> The true bride waits for you."

He looked down at her foot and saw how the blood was running out of the shoe, and how it had stained her white stocking. Then he turned his horse and took the false bride home again. "This also is not the right one," said he. "Have you no other daughter?"

"No," said the man. "There is still a little stunted kitchen wench that my late wife left behind her, but she cannot possibly be the bride."

The king's son said he was to send her up to him, but the mother answered, "Oh, no, she is much too dirty, she cannot show herself!"

He absolutely insisted on it, and Cinderella had to be called. She first washed her hands and face clean, and then went and bowed down before the king's son, who gave her the golden shoe. Then she seated herself on a stool, drew her foot out of the heavy wooden shoe, and put it into the slipper, which fitted like a glove. When she rose up and the king's son looked at her face, he recognized the beautiful maiden who had danced with him and he cried, "That is the true bride!" The stepmother and the two sisters were terrified and became pale with rage; he, however, took Cinderella on his horse and rode away with her. As they passed by the hazel tree, the two white doves cried,

"Turn and peep, turn and peep,
No blood is in the shoe,
The shoe is not too small for her,
The true bride rides with you."

And when they had cried that, the two came flying down and placed themselves on Cinderella's shoulders, one on the right, the other on the left, and remained sitting there.

When the wedding with the king's son had to be celebrated, the two false sisters came and wanted to get into favor with Cinderella and share her good fortune. When the betrothed couple went to church, the elder was at the right side and the younger at the left, and the pigeons pecked out one eye of each of them. Afterward as they came back, the elder was at the left, and the younger at the right, and then the pigeons pecked out the other eye of each. And thus, for their wickedness and falsehood, they were punished with blindness as long as they lived.

The White Snake

A LONG TIME AGO THERE lived a king who was famed for his wisdom through all the land. Nothing was hidden from him, and it seemed as if news of the most secret things was brought to him through the air. But he had a strange custom; every day after dinner, when the table was cleared and no one else was present, a trusty servant had to bring him one more dish. It was covered, however, and even the servant did not know what was in it; neither did anyone know, for the king never took off the cover to eat of it until he was quite alone.

This had gone on for a long time, when one day the servant who took away the dish was overcome with such curiosity that he could not help carrying the dish into his room. When he had carefully locked the door, he lifted up the cover and saw a white snake lying on the dish. But when he saw it he could not deny himself the pleasure of tasting it, so he cut off a little bit and put it into his mouth. No sooner had it touched his tongue than he heard a strange whispering of little voices outside his window. He went and listened, and then noticed that it was the sparrows who were chattering together, telling one another of all kinds of things that they had seen in the fields and woods. Eating the snake had given him power of understanding the language of animals.

Now it so happened that on this very day the queen lost her most beautiful ring, and suspicion of having stolen it fell upon this trusty servant, who was allowed to go everywhere. The king ordered the man to be brought before him, and threatened with angry words that unless he could before the morrow point out the thief, he himself should be looked upon as guilty and executed. In vain he declared his innocence; he was dismissed with no better answer.

In his trouble and fear he went down into the courtyard and took thought how to help himself out of his trouble. Now, some ducks were sitting together quietly by a brook and taking their rest; and, while they were making their feathers smooth with their bills, they were having a confidential conversation together. The servant stood by and listened. They were telling one another of all the places where they had been waddling about all the morning, and what good food they had found, and one said in a pitiful tone, "Something lies heavy on my stomach; as I was eating in haste, I swallowed a ring that lay under the queen's window."

The servant at once seized her by the neck, carried

her to the kitchen, and said to the cook, "Here is a fine duck; pray, kill her."

"Yes," said the cook, and weighed her in his hand. "She has spared no trouble to fatten herself and has been waiting to be roasted long enough." So he cut off her head, and as she was being dressed for the spit, the queen's ring was found inside her.

The servant could now easily prove his innocence; and the king, to make amends for the wrong, allowed him to ask a favor, and promised him the best place in the court that he could wish for. The servant refused everything, and only asked for a horse and some money for traveling, as he had a mind to see the world and go about a little.

When his request was granted he set out on his way, and one day came to a pond, where he saw three fishes caught in the reeds and gasping for water. Now, though it is said that fishes are dumb, he heard them lamenting that they must perish so miserably, and, as he had a kind heart, he got off his horse and put the three prisoners back into the water. They quivered with delight, put out their heads, and cried to him, "We will remember you and repay you for saving us!"

He rode on, and after a while it seemed to him that he heard a voice in the sand at his feet. He listened, and heard an ant queen complain, "Why cannot folks, with their clumsy beasts, keep off our bodies? That stupid horse, with his heavy hooves, has been treading down my people without mercy!" So he turned onto a side path and the ant queen cried out to him, "We will remember you—one good turn deserves another!"

The path led him into a wood, and here he saw two old ravens standing by their nest and throwing out their young ones. "Out with you, you idle, good-for-nothing creatures!" cried they. "We cannot find food for you any longer; you are big enough and can provide for yourselves."

But the poor young ravens lay upon the ground, flapping their wings and crying, "Oh, what helpless chicks we are! We must shift for ourselves, and yet we cannot fly! What can we do but lie here and starve?" So the good young fellow alighted, killed his horse with his sword, and gave it to them for food. Then they came hopping up to it, satisfied their hunger, and cried, "We will remember you—one good turn deserves another!"

And now he had to use his own legs. When he had walked a long way, he came to a large city. There was a great noise and crowd in the streets, and a man rode up on horseback, crying aloud, "The king's daughter wants a husband; but whoever sues for her hand must perform a hard task, and if he does not succeed, he will forfeit his life." Many had already made the attempt, but in vain; nevertheless when the youth saw the king's daughter he was so overcome by her great beauty that he forgot all danger, went before the king, and declared himself a suitor.

So he was led out to the sea, and a gold ring was thrown into it, in his sight; then the king ordered him to fetch this ring up from the bottom of the sea, and added, "If you come up again without it, you will be thrown in again and again until you perish amid the waves." All the people grieved for the handsome youth; then they went away, leaving him alone by the sea.

He stood on the shore and considered what he should do, when suddenly he saw three fishes come swimming toward him. They were the very fishes whose lives he had saved. The one in the middle held a mussel in its mouth, which it laid on the shore at the youth's feet. When he had taken it up and opened it, there lay the gold ring in the shell. Full of joy, he took it to the king and expected that he would grant him the promised reward.

But when the proud princess perceived that he was not her equal in birth, she scorned him, and required him first to perform another task. She went down into the garden and strewed with her own hands ten sacks full of millet seed on the grass; then she said, "Tomorrow morning before sunrise these must be picked up, and not a single grain be wanting."

The youth sat down in the garden and considered how it might be possible to perform this task, but he could think of nothing, and there he sat sorrowfully awaiting the break of day, when he should be led to death. But as soon as the first rays of the sun shone into the garden he saw all the ten sacks standing side by side, quite full, and not a single grain was missing. The ant queen had come in the night with thousands and thousands of ants, and the grateful creatures had by great industry picked up all the millet seed and gathered them into the sacks.

Presently the king's daughter herself came down into the garden and was amazed to see that the young man had done the task she had given him. But she could not yet conquer her proud heart, and said, "Although he has performed both the tasks, he shall not be my husband until he has brought me an apple from the Tree of Life."

The youth did not know where the Tree of Life stood, but he set out, and would have gone on forever, as long as his legs would carry him, though he had no hope of finding it. After he had wandered through three kingdoms, he came one evening to a wood, and lay down under a tree to sleep. But he heard a rustling in the branches, and a golden apple fell into his hand. At the same time three ravens flew down to him, perched themselves upon his knee, and said, "We are the three young ravens whom you saved from starving; when we had grown big, and heard that you were seeking the Golden Apple, we flew over the sea to the end of the world, where the Tree of Life stands, and have brought you the apple." The youth, full of joy, set out homeward, and took the Golden Apple to the king's beautiful daughter, who had no more excuses left to make. They cut the Apple of Life in two and ate it together; and then her heart became full of love for him, and they lived in undisturbed happiness to a great age.

The Elves and the Shoemaker

A SHOEMAKER, BY NO FAULT of his own, had become so poor that at last he had nothing left but leather for one pair of shoes. So in the evening, he cut out the shoes that he wished to begin to make the next morning, and as he had a good conscience, he lay down quietly in his bed, commended himself to God, and fell asleep. In the morning, after he had said his prayers and was just going to sit down to work, the two shoes stood quite finished on his table. He was astounded and knew not what to say to it. He took the shoes in his hands to observe them closer, and they were so neatly made that there was not one bad stitch in them, just as if they were intended as a masterpiece.

Soon after, a buyer came in, and as the shoes pleased him so well, he paid more for them than was customary, and, with the money, the shoemaker was able to purchase leather for two pairs of shoes. He cut them out at night, and next morning was about to set to work with fresh courage; but he had no need to do so, for, when he got up, they were already made, and he wanted not for buyers, who gave him money enough to buy leather for four pairs of shoes. The following morning, too, he found the four pairs made. And so it went on constantly, what he cut out in the evening was finished by the morning, so that he soon had his honest independence again, and at last became a wealthy man.

Now it befell that one evening not long before Christmas, when the man had been cutting out, he said to his wife, before going to bed, "What think you if we were to stay up tonight to see who it is that lends us this helping hand?" The woman liked the idea, and lighted a candle, and then they hid themselves in a corner of the room, behind some clothes that were hanging up there, and watched. When it was midnight, two pretty little naked men came, sat down by the shoemaker's table, took all the work that was cut out before them, and began to stitch, sew, and hammer so skillfully and so quickly with their little fingers that the shoemaker could not turn away his eyes for astonishment. They did not stop until all was done and stood finished on the table, and they ran quickly away.

Next morning the woman said, "The little men have made us rich, and we really must show that we are grateful for it. They run about so and have nothing on, and must be cold. I'll tell thee what I'll do: I will make them little shirts, and coats, and vests, and trousers, and knit both of them a pair of stockings, and do thou, too; make them two little pairs of shoes."

The man said, "I shall be very glad to do it," and one night, when everything was ready, they laid their presents all together on the table instead of the cutout work, then concealed themselves to see how the little men would behave. At midnight they came bounding in and wanted to get to work at once, but as they did not find any leather cut out, but only the pretty little articles of clothing, they were at first astonished, and then they showed intense delight. They dressed themselves with the greatest rapidity, putting the pretty clothes on and singing,

"Now we are boys so fine to see,
Why should we longer cobblers be?"

Then they danced and skipped and leapt over chairs and benches. At last they danced out of doors. From that time forth they came no more, but as long as the shoemaker lived all went well with him, and all his undertakings prospered.

The Peasant's Clever Daughter

THERE WAS ONCE A POOR peasant who had no land, but only a small house and one daughter. Said the daughter, "We ought to ask our lord the king for a bit of newly cleared land." When the king heard of their poverty, he presented them with a piece of land, which she and her father dug up and intended to sow with a little corn and grain of that kind. When they had dug nearly the whole of the field, they found in the earth a mortar made of pure gold.

"Listen," said the father to the girl. "As our lord the king has been so gracious and presented us with the field, we ought to give him this mortar in return for it."

The daughter, however, would not consent to this, and said, "Father, if we have the mortar without having the pestle as well, we shall have to get the pestle, so you had much better say nothing about it."

He would, however, not obey her, but took the mortar and carried it to the king. He said that he had found it in the cleared land, and asked if he would accept it as a present. The king took the mortar and asked if he had found nothing besides that. "No," answered the country-man. Then the king said that he must now bring him the pestle. The peasant said they had not found that, but he might just as well have spoken to the wind; he was put in prison and was to stay there until he produced the pestle.

The servants had daily to carry him bread and water, which is what people get in prison, and they heard how the man cried out continually, "Ah! If I had but listened to my daughter! Alas, alas, if I had but listened to my daughter!" and would neither eat nor drink. So the king commanded the servants to bring the prisoner before him, and then he asked the peasant why he was always crying "Ah! If I had but listened to my daughter!" and what it was that his daughter had said. "She told me that I ought not to take the mortar to you, for I should have to produce the pestle as well."

"If you have a daughter who is as wise as that, let her come here." She was therefore obliged to appear before the king, who asked her if she really was so wise, and said he would set her a riddle, and if she could guess that, he would marry her. She at once said yes, she would guess it. Then said the king, "Come to me not clothed, not naked, not riding, not walking, not in the road, and not out of the road, and if thou canst do that, I will marry thee."

So she went away, took off everything she had on, and then she was not clothed, took a great fishing net, and seated herself in it and wrapped it entirely around and around her so that she was not naked. She hired a donkey and tied the fisherman's net to its tail so that it was forced to drag her along, and that was neither riding nor walking. The donkey had also to drag her in the ruts, so that she only touched the ground with her great toe, and that was neither being in the road nor out of the road. And when she arrived in that fashion, the king said she had guessed the riddle and fulfilled all the conditions. Then he ordered her father to be released from the prison, took her to wife, and gave into her care all the royal possessions.

Now once when some years had passed, the king was drawing up his troops on parade, when it happened that some peasants who had been selling wood stopped with their wagons before the palace; some of them had oxen yoked to them, and some horses. There was one peasant who had three horses, one of which was delivered of a young foal, which ran away and lay down between two oxen that were in front of the wagon. When the peasants came together, they began to dispute, to beat one another, and make a disturbance. The peasant with the oxen wanted to keep the foal, and said one of the oxen had given birth to it; the other said his horse had had it, and that it was his.

The quarrel came before the king, and he give the verdict that the foal should stay where it had been found, so the peasant with the oxen, to whom it did not belong, got it. Then the other went away and wept and lamented over his foal. Now, he had heard how gracious his lady the queen was because she herself had sprung from poor peasant folks, so he went to her and begged her to see if she could not help him to get his foal back again. Said she, "Yes, I will tell you what to do, if thou wilt promise me not to betray me. Early tomorrow morning, when the king parades the guard, place thyself there in the middle of the road by which he must pass, take a great fishing net, and pretend to be fishing. Go on fishing, too, and empty out the net as if thou hadst got it full." Then she told him also what he was to say if he was questioned by the king.

The next day, therefore, the peasant stood there and fished on dry ground. When the king passed by and saw that, he sent his messenger to ask what the stupid man was about. He answered, "I am fishing." The messenger asked how he could fish when there was no water there. The peasant said, "It is as easy for me to fish on dry land as it is for an ox to have a foal." The messenger went back and took the answer to the king, who ordered the peasant to be brought to him. The king told him that this was not his own idea, and he wanted to know whose it was. The peasant must confess this at once. The peasant, however, would not do so, and said always—God forbid he should!—the idea was his own. They laid him, however, on a heap of straw, and beat him and tormented him so long that at last he admitted that he had gotten the idea from the queen.

When the king reached home again, he said to his wife, "Why hast thou behaved so falsely to me? I will not have thee any longer for a wife; thy time is up, go back to the place from whence thou camest, to thy peasant's hut."

One favor, however, he granted her; she might take with her the one thing that was dearest and best in her eyes. Thus was she dismissed. She said, "Yes, my dear husband, if you command this, I will do it," and she embraced him and kissed him, and said she would take leave of him. Then she ordered a powerful sleeping draft to be brought to drink farewell to him; the king took a long draft, but she took only a little. He soon fell into a deep sleep, and when she perceived that, she called a servant, took a fair white linen cloth, and wrapped the king in it.

The servant was forced to carry the king into a carriage that stood before the door, and the queen drove with him to her own little house. She laid him in her own little bed, and he slept one day and one night without awakening. When he awoke he looked around and said, "Good God! Where am I?" He called his attendants, but none of them were there.

At length his wife came to his bedside and said, "My dear lord and king, you told me I might bring away with me from the palace that which was dearest and most precious in my eyes; I have nothing more precious and dear than yourself, so I have brought you with me."

Tears rose to the king's eyes and he said, "Dear wife, thou shalt be mine and I will be thine." He took her back with him to the royal palace and was married again to her, and at the present time they are very likely still living.

Rumpelstiltskin

ONCE THERE WAS A MILLER who was poor, but who had a beautiful daughter. Now it happened that he had to go and speak to the king, and in order to make himself appear important he said to him, "I have a daughter who can spin straw into gold."

The king said to the miller, "That is an art which pleases me well; if your daughter is as clever as you say, bring her tomorrow to my palace, and I will try what she can do."

When the girl was brought to him he took her into a room that was quite full of straw, gave her a spinning wheel and a reel, and said, "Now set to work, and if by tomorrow morning early you have not spun this straw into gold during the night, you must die." Thereupon he himself locked up the room and left her in it alone. So there sat the poor miller's daughter, and for the life of her could not tell what to do; she had no idea how straw could be spun into gold, and she grew more and more miserable, until at last she began to weep.

But all at once the door opened, and in came a little

man, who said, "Good evening, Mistress Miller; why are you crying so?"

"Alas!" answered the girl. "I have to spin straw into gold, and I do not know how to do it."

"What will you give me," said the little man, "if I do it for you?"

"My necklace," said the girl.

The little man took the necklace, seated himself in front of the wheel, and whirr, whirr, whirr, three turns, and the reel was full; then he put another on, and whirr, whirr, whirr, three times round, and the second was full, too. And so it went on until the morning, when all the straw was spun, and all the reels were full of gold.

By daybreak the king was already there, and when he saw the gold he was astonished and delighted, but his heart became only more greedy. He had the miller's daughter taken into another room full of straw, which was much larger, and commanded her to spin that also in one night if she valued her life. The girl knew not how to help herself and was crying when the door again opened, and the little man appeared and said, "What will you give me if I spin that straw into gold for you?"

"The ring on my finger," answered the girl.

The little man took the ring, again began to turn the wheel, and by morning had spun all the straw into glittering gold.

The king rejoiced beyond measure at the sight, but still he had not gold enough; he had the miller's daughter taken into a still larger room full of straw and said, "You must spin this, too, in the course of this night; but if you succeed, you shall be my wife." *Even if she be a miller's daughter*, thought he, *I could not find a richer wife in the whole world.*

When the girl was alone, the little man came again for the third time and said, "What will you give me if I spin the straw for you this time also?"

"I have nothing left that I could give," answered the girl.

"Then promise me, if you should become queen, your first child."

Who knows whether that will ever happen? thought the miller's daughter; and, not knowing how else to help herself in this strait, she promised the little man what he wanted, and for that he once more span the straw into gold.

When the king came in the morning and found all as he had wished, he took her in marriage, and the pretty miller's daughter became a queen.

A year after, she had a beautiful child, and she never gave a thought to the little man. But suddenly he came into her room and said, "Now give me what you promised." The queen was horror-struck, and offered the little man all the riches of the kingdom if he would leave her the child. But the little man said, "No, something that is living is dearer to me than all the treasures in the world." Then the queen began to weep and cry, so that the little man pitied her. "I will give you three days' time," said he. "If by that time you find out my name, then shall you keep your child."

So the queen thought the whole night of all the names that she had ever heard, and she sent a messenger over the country to inquire, far and wide, for any other names that there might be. When the little man came the next day, she began with Caspar, Melchior, Balthazar, and said all the names she knew, one after another; but to everyone the little man said, "That is not my name."

On the second day she had inquiries made in the neighborhood as to the names of the people there, and she repeated to the little man the most uncommon and curious. "Perhaps your name is Shortribs, or Sheepshanks, or Laceleg?"

But he always answered, "That is not my name."

On the third day the messenger came back again and said, "I have not been able to find a single new name, but as I came to a high mountain at the end of the forest, where the fox and the hare bid each other good night, there I saw a little house. Before the house a fire was burning, and around about the fire quite a ridiculous little man was jumping: He hopped upon one leg, and shouted,

"Today I bake, tomorrow brew,
The next I'll have the young queen's child.
Ha! Glad am I that no one knew
That Rumpelstiltskin I am styled."

You may think how glad the queen was when she heard the name! Soon afterward the little man came in and asked, "Now, Mistress Queen, what is my name?"

At first she said, "Is your name Conrad?"

"No."

"Is your name Harry?"

"No."

"Perhaps your name is Rumpelstiltskin?"

"The devil has told you that! The devil has told you that!" cried the little man, and in his anger he plunged his right foot so deep into the earth that his whole leg went in; then in rage he pulled at his left leg so hard with both hands that he tore himself in two.

The Twelve Dancing Princesses

THERE WAS ONCE UPON A TIME a king who had twelve daughters, each one more beautiful than the other. They all slept together in one chamber, in which their beds stood side by side, and every night when they were in them the king locked the door and bolted it. But in the morning when he unlocked the door, he saw that their shoes were worn out with dancing, and no one could find out how that had come to pass. Then the king caused it to be proclaimed that whosoever could discover where they danced at night should choose one of them for his wife and be king after his death, but that whosoever came forward and had not discovered it within three days and nights should have forfeited his life.

It was not long before a prince presented himself and offered to undertake the enterprise. He was well received, and in the evening was led into a room adjoining the princesses' sleeping chamber. His bed was placed there, and he was to observe where they went and danced, and in order that they might do nothing secretly or go away to some other place, the door of their room was left open.

But the eyelids of the prince grew heavy as lead, and he fell asleep. When he awoke in the morning, all twelve had been to the dance, for their shoes were standing there with holes in the soles. On the second and third nights it fell out just the same, and then his head was struck off without mercy. Many others came after this and undertook the enterprise, but all forfeited their lives.

Now it came to pass that a poor soldier, who had a wound and could serve no longer, found himself on the road to the town where the king lived. There he met an old woman, who asked him where he was going. "I hardly know myself," answered he, and added in jest, "I had half a mind to discover where the princesses danced their shoes into holes, and thus become king."

"That is not so difficult," said the old woman. "You must not drink the wine that will be brought to you at night and must pretend to be sound asleep." With that she gave him a little cloak and said, "If you put on that, you will be invisible, and then you can steal after the twelve."

When the soldier had received this good advice, he went into the thing in earnest, took heart, went to the king, and announced himself as a suitor. He was as well received as the others, and royal garments were put upon him. He was conducted that evening at bedtime into the antechamber, and as he was about to go to bed, the eldest came and brought him a cup of wine. But he had tied a sponge under his chin, and let the wine run down into it without drinking a drop. Then he lay down and when he had lain a while, he began to snore, as if in the deepest sleep. The twelve princesses heard that and laughed, and the eldest said, "He, too, might as well have saved his life."

With that they got up, opened wardrobes and cupboards, and brought out pretty dresses. They dressed themselves before the mirrors, sprang about, and rejoiced at the prospect of the dance. Only the youngest said, "I know not how it is; you are very happy, but I feel very strange; some misfortune is certainly about to befall us."

"Thou art a goose, who art always frightened," said the eldest. "Hast thou forgotten how many kings' sons have already come here in vain? I had hardly any need to give the soldier a sleeping draft; in any case the clown would not have awakened." When they were all ready they looked carefully at the soldier, but he had closed his eyes and did not move or stir, so they felt themselves quite secure. The eldest then went to her bed and tapped it; it immediately sank into the earth, and one after the other they descended through the opening, the eldest going first. The soldier, who had watched everything, tarried no longer. He put on his little cloak and went down last with the youngest.

Halfway down the steps, he trod just a little on her dress; she was terrified at that, and cried out, "What is that? Who is pulling my dress?"

"Don't be so silly!" said the eldest. "You have caught it on a nail."

Then they went all the way down, and when they were at the bottom, they were standing in a wonderfully pretty avenue of trees, all the leaves of which were of silver, and shone and glistened. The soldier thought, *I must carry a token away with me*, and broke off a twig from one of them, upon which the tree cracked with a loud report.

The youngest cried out again. "Something is wrong; did you hear the crack?"

But the eldest said, "It is a gun fired for joy, because we have gotten rid of our prince so quickly." After that they came into an avenue where all the leaves were of gold, and lastly into a third where they were of bright diamonds; he broke off a twig from each, which made such a crack each time that the youngest started back in terror, but the eldest still maintained that they were salutes.

They went on and came to a great lake whereon stood twelve little boats, and in every boat sat a handsome prince, all of whom were waiting for the twelve. Each took one of them with him, but the soldier seated himself by the youngest. Then her prince said, "I can't tell why the boat is so much heavier today; I shall have to row with all my strength if I am to get it across."

"What should cause that," said the youngest, "but the warm weather? I feel very warm, too." On the opposite side of the lake stood a splendid, brightly lit castle, from whence resounded the joyous music of trumpets and kettledrums. They rowed over there, entered, and each prince danced with the girl he loved. The soldier danced with them unseen, and when one of them had a cup of wine in her hand he drank it up, so that the cup was empty when she carried it to her mouth; the youngest was alarmed at this, but the eldest always made her be silent. They danced there till three o'clock in the morning, when all the shoes were danced into holes and they were forced to leave off; the princes rowed them back again over the lake, and this time the soldier seated himself by the eldest.

On the shore they took leave of their princes and promised to return the following night. When they reached the stairs, the soldier ran on in front and lay down in his bed, and when the twelve had come up slowly and wearily, he was already snoring so loudly that they could all hear him, and they said, "So far as he is concerned, we are safe." They took off their beautiful dresses, laid them away, put the worn-out shoes under their beds, and lay down.

The next morning, the soldier was resolved not to speak, but to watch the wonderful goings on, and again went with them. Then everything was done just as it had been done the first time, and each time they danced until their shoes were worn to pieces. But the third time, he took a cup away with him as a token. When the hour had arrived for him to give his answer, he took the three twigs and the cup and went to the king, but the twelve stood behind the door and listened for what he was going to say.

The king put the question, "Where have my twelve daughters danced their shoes to pieces in the night?"

The soldier answered, "In an underground castle with twelve princes." Then he related how it had come to pass and brought out the tokens. The king then summoned his daughters and asked them if the soldier had told the truth; when they saw that they were betrayed, and that falsehood would be of no avail, they were obliged to confess all. Thereupon the king asked which of them he would have to wife. He answered, "I am no longer young, so give me the eldest." Then the wedding was celebrated on the selfsame day, and the kingdom was promised him after the king's death. But the princes were bewitched for as many days as they had danced nights with the twelve.

The Six Swans

ONCE UPON A TIME, a certain king was hunting in a great forest, and he chased a wild beast so eagerly that none of his attendants could follow him. When evening drew near he stopped and looked around him, and then he saw that he had lost his way. He sought a way out, but could find none. Then he perceived an aged woman with a head that nodded perpetually, who came toward him, but she was a witch.

"Good woman," said he to her. "Can you not show me the way through the forest?"

"Oh, yes, Lord King," she answered, "that I certainly can, but on one condition, and if you do not fulfill that, you will never get out of the forest, and will die of hunger in it."

"What kind of condition is it?" asked the king.

"I have a daughter," said the old woman, "who is as beautiful as anyone in the world, and well deserves to be your consort. If you will make her your queen, I will show you the way out of the forest." In the anguish of his heart the king consented, and the old woman led him to her little hut, where her daughter was sitting by the fire. She received the king as if she had been expecting him, and he saw that she was very beautiful, but still she did not please him, and he could not look at her without secret horror. After he had taken the maiden up on his horse, the old woman showed him the way, and the king reached his royal palace again, where the wedding was celebrated.

The king had already been married once and had by his first wife seven children: six boys and a girl, whom he loved better than anything else in the world. As he now feared that the stepmother might not treat them well, and even do them some injury, he took them to a lonely castle that stood in the midst of a forest. It lay so concealed, and the way was so difficult to find, that he himself would not have found it, if a wise woman had not given him a ball of yarn with wonderful properties. When he threw it down before him, it unrolled itself and showed him his path. The king, however, went so frequently away to his dear children that the queen observed his absence; she was curious and wanted to know what he did when he was quite alone in the forest. She gave a great deal of money to his servants, and they betrayed the secret to her, and told her likewise of the ball, which alone could point out the way.

Now she knew no rest until she had learnt where the king kept the ball of yarn, and then she made little shirts of white silk, and as she had learnt the art of witchcraft from her mother, she sewed a charm inside them. Once when the king had ridden forth to hunt, she took the little shirts and went into the forest, and the ball showed her the way. The children, who saw from a distance that someone was approaching, thought that their dear father was coming to them, and full of joy, they ran to meet him. Then she threw one of the little shirts over each of them, and no sooner had the shirts touched their bodies than they were changed into swans and flew away over the forest.

The queen went home quite delighted and thought she had gotten rid of her stepchildren. But the girl had not run out with her brothers, and the queen knew nothing about her. Next day, the king went to visit his children, but he found no one but the little girl. "Where are thy brothers?" asked the king.

"Alas, dear father," she answered, "they have gone away and left me alone!" She told him that she had seen from her little window how her brothers had flown away over the forest in the shape of swans, and she showed him the feathers that they had let fall in the courtyard, which she had picked up.

The king mourned, but he did not think that the queen had done this wicked deed, and as he feared that the girl would also be stolen away from him, he wanted to take her away with him. But she was afraid of her stepmother, and entreated the king to let her stay just this one night more in the forest castle.

The poor girl thought, *I can no longer stay here. I will go and seek my brothers.* When night came, she ran away and went straight into the forest. She walked the whole night long and the next day also without stopping, until she could go no farther for weariness. Then she saw a forest hut, went into it, and found a room with six little beds. She did not venture to get into one of them but crept under one and lay down on the hard ground, intending to pass the night there.

Just before sunset, however, she heard a rustling, and saw six swans come flying in at the window. They alighted on the ground and blew at each other, and blew all the feathers off, and their swan's skins stripped off like a shirt. Then the maiden looked at them and recognized her brothers; she was glad and crept forth from beneath the bed.

The brothers were not less delighted to see their little sister, but their joy was of short duration. "Here canst thou not abide," they said to her. "This is a shelter for robbers; if they come home and find thee, they will kill thee."

"But can you not protect me?" asked the little sister.

"No," they replied. "Only for one quarter of an hour

each evening can we lay aside our swan's skins and have during that time our human form; after that, we are once more turned into swans."

The little sister wept and said, "Can you not be set free?"

"Alas, no," they answered. "The conditions are too hard! For six years thou mayst neither speak nor laugh, and in that time thou must sew together six little shirts of starwort for us. And if one single word falls from thy lips, all thy work will be lost." When the brothers had said this, the quarter of an hour was over, and they flew out of the window again as swans.

The maiden, however, firmly resolved to deliver her brothers, even if it should cost her her life. She left the hut, went into the midst of the forest, seated herself on a tree, and there passed the night. Next morning she went out, gathered starwort, and began to sew. She could not speak to anyone, and she had no inclination to laugh; she sat there and looked at nothing but her work.

When she had already spent a long time there, it came to pass that the king of the country* was hunting in the forest, and his huntsmen came to the tree on which the maiden was sitting. They called to her and said, "Who art thou?" But she made no answer. "Come down to us," said they. "We will not do thee any harm."

*A different king, who was not her father

She only shook her head. As they pressed her further with questions she threw her golden necklace down to them, and thought to content them thus. They, however, did not cease, and then she threw her girdle down to them, and as this also was to no purpose, her garters, and by degrees everything that she had on that she could do without until she had nothing left but her shift.

The huntsmen, however, did not let themselves be turned aside by that, but climbed the tree, fetched the maiden down, and led her before the king. The king asked, "Who art thou? What art thou doing on the tree?" But she did not answer. He put the question in every language that he knew, but she remained as mute as a fish. Since she was so beautiful, the king's heart was touched, and he was smitten with a great love for her. He put his mantle on her, took her before him on his horse, and carried her to his castle. Then he caused her to be dressed in rich garments, and she shone in her beauty like bright daylight, but no word could be drawn from her. He placed her by his side at table, and her modest bearing and courtesy pleased him so much that he said, "She is the one whom I wish to marry, and no other woman in the world." And after some days he united himself to her.

The king, however, had a wicked mother who was

dissatisfied with this marriage and spoke ill of the young queen. "Who knows," said she, "from whence the creature who can't speak comes? She is not worthy of a king!" After a year had passed, when the queen brought her first child into the world, the old woman took it away from her and smeared her mouth with blood as she slept. Then she went to the king and accused the queen of being a man-eater. The king would not believe it and would not suffer anyone to do her any injury. She, however, sat continually sewing at the shirts and cared for nothing else.

The next time, when she again bore a beautiful boy, the false mother used the same treachery, but the king could not bring himself to give credit to her words. He said, "She is too pious and good to do anything of that kind; if she were not mute, and could defend herself, her innocence would come to light."

But when the old woman stole away the third newly born child and accused the queen, who did not utter one word of defense, the king could do no otherwise than deliver her over to justice, and she was sentenced to suffer death by fire.

When the day came for the sentence to be executed, it was the last day of the six years during which she was not to speak or laugh, and she had delivered her dear brothers from the power of the enchantment. The six shirts were ready; only the left sleeve of the sixth was wanting. When, therefore, she was led to the stake, she laid the shirts on her arm, and when she stood on high and the fire was just going to be lighted, she looked around and six swans came flying through the air toward her. Then she saw that her deliverance was near, and her heart leapt with joy. The swans swept to her and sank down so that she could throw the shirts over them, and as they were touched by them, their swan's skins fell off, and her brothers stood in their own bodily form before her, vigorous and handsome. The youngest lacked only his left arm and had in the place of it a swan's wing on his shoulder.

They embraced and kissed one another, and the queen went to the king, who was greatly moved, and she began to speak and said, "Dearest husband, now I may speak and declare to thee that I am innocent and falsely accused." She told him of the treachery of the old woman who had taken away her three children and hidden them. Then to the great joy of the king the children were brought thither, and as a punishment, the king's wicked mother was bound to the stake and burnt to ashes. But the king and the queen with her six brothers lived many years in happiness and peace.

The Goose Girl

THERE WAS ONCE UPON A TIME an old queen whose husband had been dead for many years, and she had a beautiful daughter. When the princess grew up, she was betrothed to a prince who lived at a great distance. When the time came for her to be married, and she had to journey forth into the distant kingdom, the aged queen packed up for her many costly vessels of silver and gold, and trinkets also of gold and silver, and cups and jewels—in short, everything that appertained to a royal dowry, for she loved her child with all her heart.

She likewise sent her maid-in-waiting, who was to ride with her and hand her over to the bridegroom. Each had a horse for the journey, but the horse of the king's daughter was called Falada, and could speak. So when the hour of parting had come, the aged mother went into her bedroom, took a small knife, and cut her finger with it until it bled. Then she held a white handkerchief to it into where she let three drops of blood fall, gave it to her daughter, and said, "Dear child, preserve this carefully; it will be of service to you on your way."

So they took a sorrowful leave of each other; the

princess put the piece of cloth in the bosom of her dress, mounted her horse, and then went on her way to her bridegroom. After she had ridden for a while she felt a burning thirst, and said to her waiting-maid, "Dismount, take my cup which thou hast brought with thee for me, and get me some water from the stream, for I should like to drink."

"If you are thirsty," said the waiting-maid, "get off your horse yourself, and lie down and drink out of the water. I don't choose to be your servant."

So in her great thirst the princess alighted, bent down over the water in the stream, and drank, and was not allowed to drink out of the golden cup. Then she said, "Ah, Heaven!"

And the three drops of blood answered, "If thy mother knew, her heart would break."

But the king's daughter was humble, said nothing, and mounted her horse again. She rode some miles farther, but the day was warm, the sun scorched her, and she was thirsty once more. When they came to a stream of water, she again cried to her waiting-maid, "Dismount, and give me some water in my golden cup," for she had long ago forgotten the girl's ill words.

But the waiting-maid said still more haughtily, "If you wish to drink, drink as you can; I don't choose to be your servant."

Then in her great thirst the king's daughter alighted, bent over the flowing stream, wept, and said, "Ah, Heaven!"

The drops of blood again replied, "If thy mother knew this, her heart would break."

As she was thus drinking and leaning right over the stream, the handkerchief with the three drops of blood fell out of the bosom of her dress and floated away with the water without her observing it, so great was her trouble. The waiting-maid, however, had seen it, and she rejoiced to think that she now had power over the bride, for since the princess had lost the drops of blood, she had become weak and powerless. So now when the princess wanted to mount her horse again, the one that was called Falada, the waiting-maid said, "Falada is more suitable for me, and my nag will do for thee," and the princess had to be content with that. Then the waiting-maid, with many hard words, bade the princess exchange her royal apparel for her own shabby clothes; and at length she compelled the princess to swear by the clear sky above her that she would not say one word of this to anyone at the royal court, and if she had not taken this oath, she would have been killed on the spot. But Falada saw all this, and observed it well.

The waiting-maid now mounted Falada, and the true bride the bad horse, and thus they traveled onward, until at length they entered the royal palace. There were great rejoicings over her arrival, and the prince sprang forward to meet the waiting-maid, lifted her from her horse, and thought she was his consort. She was conducted upstairs, but the real princess was left standing below.

Then the old king looked out of the window and saw her standing in the courtyard, and saw how dainty and delicate and beautiful she was. He instantly went to the royal apartment and asked the bride about the girl she had with her, and asked who she was. "I picked her up on my way for a companion; give the girl something to work at, that she may not stand idle."

But the old king had no work for her, and knew of none, so he said, "I have a little boy who tends the geese; she may help him." The boy was called Conrad, and the true bride had to help him to tend the geese.

Soon afterward, the false bride said to the young king, "Dearest husband, I beg you to do me a favor."

He answered, "I will do so most willingly."

"Then send for the stable master, and have the head of the horse on which I rode here cut off, for it vexed me on the way." In reality, she was afraid that the horse might tell how she had behaved to the true bride. Then she succeeded in making the young king promise that it should be done, and the faithful Falada was to die.

This came to the ears of the real princess, and she secretly promised to pay the stable master a piece of gold if he would perform a small service for her. There was a great dark-looking gateway in the town, through which morning and evening she had to pass with the geese: Would he be so good as to nail up Falada's head on it, so that she might see him again, more than once? The stable master's man promised to do that, cut off the head, and nailed it fast beneath the dark gateway.

Early in the morning, when she and Conrad drove out their flock beneath this gateway, she said in passing,

"Alas, Falada, hanging there!"

Then the head answered,

"Alas, young queen, how ill you fare!
If this your tender mother knew,
Her heart would surely break in two."

Then they went still farther out of the town and drove their geese into the country. When they had come to the meadow, she sat down and unbound her hair, which was like pure gold. Conrad saw it and delighted in its brightness, and wanted to pluck out a few hairs. Then she said,

"Blow, blow, thou gentle wind, I say,
Blow Conrad's little hat away,
And make him chase it here and there,

Until I have braided all my hair,
And bound it up again."

And there came such a violent wind that it blew Conrad's hat far away across country, and he was forced to run after it. When he came back she had finished combing her hair and was putting it up again, and he could not get any of it. Then Conrad was angry and would not speak to her; thus they watched the geese until the evening, and then they went home.

Next day, when they were driving the geese out through the dark gateway, the maiden said,

"Alas, Falada, hanging there!"

Falada answered,

"Alas, young queen, how ill you fare!
If this your tender mother knew,
Her heart would surely break in two."

And she sat down again in the field and began to comb out her hair. Conrad ran and tried to clutch it, so she said in haste,

"Blow, blow, thou gentle wind, I say,
Blow Conrad's little hat away,
And make him chase it here and there,
Until I have braided all my hair,
And bound it up again."

Then the wind blew, and blew his little hat off his

head and far away, and Conrad was forced to run after it. When he came back, her hair had been put up a long time and he could get none of it, so they looked after their geese till evening came.

But in the evening after they had gotten home, Conrad went to the old king and said, "I won't tend the geese with that girl any longer!"

"Why not?" inquired the aged king.

"Oh, because she vexes me the whole day long." Then the aged king commanded him to relate what it was that she did to him. And Conrad said, "In the morning when we pass beneath the dark gateway with the flock, there is a sorry horse's head on the wall, and she says to it,

"'Alas, Falada, hanging there!'

"And the head replies,

"'Alas, young queen, how ill you fare!
If this your tender mother knew,
Her heart would surely break in two.'"

And Conrad went on to relate what happened on the goose pasture, and how when there, he had to chase his hat.

The aged king commanded him to drive his flock out again the next day, and as soon as morning came, he placed himself behind the dark gateway and heard how the maiden spoke to the head of Falada. Then he, too, went into the country and hid himself in the thicket in the meadow. There he soon saw with his own eyes the goose girl and the goose boy bringing their flock, and how after a while she sat down and unbraided her hair, which shone with radiance. And soon she said,

"Blow, blow, thou gentle wind, I say,
Blow Conrad's little hat away,
And make him chase it here and there,
Until I have braided all my hair,
And bound it up again."

Then came a blast of wind and carried off Conrad's hat so that he had to run far away, while the maiden quietly went on combing and plaiting her hair—all of which the king observed. Then, quite unseen, he went away, and when the goose girl came home in the evening, he called her aside and asked why she did all these things.

"I may not tell you that, and I dare not lament my sorrows to any human being, for I have sworn not to do so by the heaven that is above me; if I had not done that, I should have lost my life."

He urged her and left her no peace, but he could draw nothing from her. Then said he, "If thou wilt not tell me anything, tell thy sorrows to the iron stove there," and he went away.

Then she crept into the iron stove, and began to weep and lament. She emptied her whole heart, and said, "Here am I deserted by the whole world, and yet I am a king's daughter, and a false waiting-maid has by force brought me to such a pass that I have been compelled to put off my royal apparel, she has taken my place with my bridegroom, and I have to perform menial service as a goose girl. If my mother did but know that, her heart would break."

The aged king, however, was standing outside by the pipe of the stove, listening to what she said and heard it. Then he came back again and bade her come out of the stove. And royal garments were placed on her, and it was marvelous how beautiful she was! The aged king summoned his son and revealed to him that he had gotten the false bride, who was only a waiting-maid, but that the true one was standing there, as the sometime goose girl.

The young king rejoiced with all his heart when he saw her beauty and youth, and a great feast was made ready, to which all the people and all good friends were invited. At the head of the table sat the bridegroom with the true bride at one side of him and the waiting-maid on the other, but the waiting-maid did not recognize the princess in her dazzling array. When they had eaten and drunk and were merry, the aged king asked the waiting-maid a riddle: What did a person deserve who had behaved in such and such a way to her master; at the same time he related the whole story, and asked what sentence such a one merited.

Then the false bride said, "She deserves no better fate than to be put in a barrel that is studded with nails, and two white horses should be harnessed to it, which will drag her along through one street after another till she is dead."

"It is thou," said the aged king, "and thou hast pronounced thine own sentence, and thus shall it be done unto thee."

And when the sentence had been carried out, the young king married his true bride, and both of them reigned over their kingdom in peace and happiness.

Snow White and Rose Red

THERE WAS ONCE A POOR widow who lived in a lonely cottage. In front of the cottage was a garden wherein stood two rose bushes, one of which bore white and the other red roses. She had two children who were like the two rose bushes: One was called Snow White, and the other Rose Red. They were as good and happy, as busy and cheerful as ever two children in the world were, only Snow White was more quiet and gentle than Rose Red. Rose Red liked better to run about in the meadows and fields seeking flowers and catching butterflies; but Snow White sat at home with her mother and helped her with her housework, or read to her when there was nothing to do.

The two sisters were so fond of each other that they always held each other by the hand when they went out together, and when Snow White said, "We will not leave each other," Rose Red answered, "Never so long as we live," and their mother would add, "What one has, she must share with the other."

They often ran about the forest alone and gathered red berries. No beasts did them any harm, but came close to them trustfully. The little hare would eat a cabbage leaf out of their hands, the doe grazed by their side, the stag leapt merrily by them, and the birds sat still upon the boughs, singing whatever they knew.

No mishap overtook them; if they had stayed too late in the forest and night came on, they laid down next to each other upon the moss and slept until morning came. Their mother knew this and had no distress on their account.

Once when they had spent the night in the woods and the dawn had roused them, they saw a beautiful child in a shining white dress sitting near their bed. He got up and looked quite kindly at them, but said nothing and went away into the forest. When they looked around they found that they had been sleeping quite close to a precipice and would certainly have fallen into it in the darkness if they had gone only a few paces farther. Their mother told them that it must have been the angel who watches over good children.

Snow White and Rose Red kept their mother's little cottage so neat that it was a pleasure to look inside it. In the summer, Rose Red took care of the house, and every morning she laid a wreath of flowers by her mother's bed before she awoke, in which was a rose from each bush. In the winter, Snow White lit the fire and hung the kettle on the mantel. The kettle was made of copper, which shone brightly. In the evening, when the snowflakes fell, the mother said, "Go, Snow White, and bolt the door," and then they sat around the hearth, the mother took her spectacles and read aloud out of a large book, and the two girls listened. Close by them lay a lamb upon the floor, and behind them upon a perch sat a white dove with its head hidden beneath its wings.

One evening, as they were thus sitting comfortably together, someone knocked at the door as if he wished to be let in. The mother said, "Quick, Rose Red, open the door; it must be a traveler who is seeking shelter." Rose Red went and pushed back the bolt, thinking that it was a poor man, but it was not; it was a bear that stretched his broad black head within the door.

Rose Red screamed and sprang back, the lamb bleated, the dove fluttered, and Snow White hid herself behind her mother's bed. But the bear began to speak and said, "Do not be afraid, I will do you no harm! I am half frozen, and only want to warm myself a little beside you."

"Poor bear," said the mother, "lie down by the fire, only take care that you do not burn your coat." Then she cried, "Snow White, Rose Red, come out; the bear will do you no harm, he means well." So they both came out, and by-and-by the lamb and dove came nearer and were not afraid of him.

The bear said, "Here, children, knock the snow out of my coat a little." So they brought the broom and swept the bear's hide clean, and he stretched himself by the fire and growled contentedly and comfortably. It was not long before they grew quite at home and played tricks with their clumsy guest. They tugged his hair with their hands, put their feet upon his back and rolled him about, or they took a hazel switch and beat him, and when he growled they laughed. But the bear took it all in good part, only when they were too rough he called out, "Leave me alive, children,

"Snowy White, Rosy Red,
Will you beat your houseguest dead?"

When it was bedtime and the others went to bed, the mother said to the bear, "You can lie there by the hearth, and then you will be safe from the cold and the bad weather." As soon as day dawned the two children let him out, and he trotted across the snow into the forest.

Henceforth the bear came every evening at the same time, laid himself down by the hearth, and let the children amuse themselves with him as much as they liked. They got so used to him that the doors were never fastened until their friend had arrived.

When spring had come and all outside was green,

the bear said one morning to Snow White, "Now I must go away, and cannot come back for the whole summer."

"Where are you going, then, dear bear?" asked Snow White.

"I must go into the forest and guard my treasures from the wicked dwarfs. In the winter, when the earth is frozen hard, they are obliged to stay below and cannot work their way through; but now, when the sun has thawed and warmed the earth, they break through it and come out to pry and steal. What once gets into their hands and in their caves does not easily see daylight again."

Snow White was quite sorry for his going away, and as she unbolted the door for him and the bear was hurrying out, he caught against the bolt and a piece of his hairy coat was torn off. It seemed to Snow White as if she had seen gold shining through it, but she was not sure about it. The bear ran away quickly and was soon out of sight behind the trees.

A short time afterward the mother sent her children into the forest to get firewood. There they found a big tree that lay felled on the ground, and close by the trunk something was jumping backward and forward in the grass, but they could not make out what it was. When they came nearer they saw a dwarf with an old, withered face and a snow-white beard a yard long. The end of the beard was caught in a crevice of the tree, and the little fellow was jumping backward and forward like a dog tied to a rope, and did not know what to do.

He glared at the girls with his fiery red eyes and cried, "Why do you stand there? Can you not come here and help me?"

"What are you about there, little man?" asked Rose Red.

"You stupid, prying goose!" answered the dwarf. "I was going to split the tree to get a little wood for cooking. The little bit of food that one of us wants gets burnt up directly with thick logs; we do not swallow so much as you coarse, greedy folk. I had just driven the wedge safely in, and everything was going as I wished; but the wretched wood was too smooth and suddenly sprang asunder, and the tree closed so quickly that I could not pull out my beautiful white beard. Now it is tight in and I cannot get away, and the silly, sleek, milk-faced things laugh! Ugh! How odious you are!"

The children tried very hard, but they could not pull the beard out, it was caught too fast. "I will run and fetch someone," said Rose Red.

"You senseless goose!" snarled the dwarf. "Why should you fetch someone? You are already two too many for me; can you not think of something better?"

"Don't be impatient," said Snow White. "I will help

you." She pulled her scissors out of her pocket and cut off the end of the beard.

As soon as the dwarf felt himself free he laid hold of a bag full of gold that lay among the roots of the tree and lifted it up, grumbling to himself, "Uncouth people, to cut off a piece of my fine beard. Bad luck to you!" Then he swung the bag upon his back and went off without even once looking at the children.

Sometime after that, Snow White and Rose Red went to catch a dish of fish. As they came near the brook they saw something like a large grasshopper jumping toward the water, as if it were going to leap in. They ran to it and found that it was the dwarf. "Where are you going?" said Rose Red. "You surely don't want to go into the water?"

"I am not such a fool!" cried the dwarf. "Don't you see that the accursed fish wants to pull me in?" The little man had been sitting there fishing, and unluckily the wind had twisted his beard with the fishing line. Just then a big fish bit, and the feeble creature had not strength to pull his beard out; the fish kept the upper hand and pulled the dwarf toward him. He held on to all the reeds and rushes, but it was of little good; he was forced to follow the movements of the fish and was in urgent danger of being dragged into the water.

The girls came just in time; they held him fast and

tried to free his beard from the line, but all in vain: Beard and line were entangled fast together. Nothing was left but to bring out the scissors and cut the beard, whereby a small part of it was lost. When the dwarf saw that, he screamed out, "Is it civil, you toadstool, to disfigure one's face? Was it not enough to clip off the end of my beard? Now you have cut off the best part of it. I cannot let myself be seen by my people. I wish you had been made to run the soles off your shoes!" Then he took out a sack of pearls that lay in the rushes, and without saying a word more he dragged it away and disappeared behind a stone.

It happened that soon afterward, the mother sent the two children to the town to buy needles and thread, and laces and ribbons. The road led them across a heath upon which huge pieces of rock lay strewn here and there. Now they noticed a large bird hovering in the air, flying slowly around and around above them; it sank lower and lower, and at last settled near a rock not far off. Directly afterward they heard a loud, piteous cry. They ran up and saw with horror that the eagle had seized their old acquaintance the dwarf and was going to carry him off.

The children, full of pity, at once took tight hold of the little man and pulled against the eagle so long that at last it let its booty go. As soon as the dwarf had recovered from his first fright he cried with his shrill voice, "Could you not have done it more carefully? You dragged at my brown coat so that it is all torn and full of holes, you helpless, clumsy creatures!" Then he took up a sack full of precious stones and slipped away again under the rock into his hole. The girls, who by this time were used to his thanklessness, went on their way and did their business in the town.

As they crossed the heath again on their way home they surprised the dwarf, who had emptied out his bag of precious stones in a clean spot and had not thought that anyone would come there so late. The evening sun shone upon the brilliant stones; they glittered and sparkled with all colors so beautifully that the children stood still and looked at them. "Why do you stand gaping there?" cried the dwarf, and his ashen-gray face became copper-red with rage. He was going on with his bad words when a loud growling was heard, and a black bear came trotting toward them out of the forest.

The dwarf sprang up in a fright, but he could not get to his cave, for the bear was already close. Then in the dread of his heart he cried, "Dear Mr. Bear, spare me, I will give you all my treasures; look, the beautiful jewels lying there! Grant me my life; what do you want with such a slender little fellow as I? You would not feel me between your teeth. Come, take these two wicked girls, they are tender morsels for you, fat as young quails; for mercy's sake eat them!" The bear took no heed of his words, but gave the dwarf a single blow with his paw, and the wicked creature did not move again.

The girls had run away, but the bear called to them, "Snow White and Rose Red, do not be afraid; wait, I will come with you." Then they knew his voice and waited, and when he came up to them suddenly his bearskin fell off, and he stood there a handsome man, clothed all in gold. "I am a king's son," he said, "and I was bewitched by that wicked dwarf, who had stolen my treasures; I have had to run about the forest as a savage bear until I was freed by his death. Now he has gotten his well-deserved punishment."

Snow White was married to him, and Rose Red to his brother, and they divided between them the great treasure that the dwarf had gathered together in his cave. The old mother lived peacefully and happily with her children for many years. She took the two rose bushes with her, and they stood before her window, and every year bore the most beautiful roses, white and red.

The Devil with the Three Golden Hairs

THERE WAS ONCE A POOR woman who gave birth to a little son; and since he came into the world with a caul still covering his head from the womb, it was predicted that in his fourteenth year he would have the king's daughter for his wife. It happened that soon afterward the king came into the village, but no one knew that he was the king. When he asked the people what news there was, they answered, "A child has just been born with a caul on; whatever anyone so born undertakes turns out well. It is prophesied, too, that in his fourteenth year he will have the king's daughter for his wife."

The king, who had a bad heart, was angry about the prophecy. He went to the parents and, seeming quite friendly, said, "You poor people, let me have your child, and I will take care of him." At first they refused, but when the stranger offered them a large amount of gold for him, they thought, *It is a luck-child, and everything must turn out well for it*, they at last consented, and gave him the child.

The king put the child in a box and rode away with

him until he came to a deep piece of water; then he threw the box into it and thought, *I have freed my daughter from her unlooked-for suitor.*

The box, however, did not sink, but floated like a boat, and not a drop of water made its way into it. It floated to within two miles of the king's chief city, where there was a mill, and it came to a standstill at the milldam. A miller's boy, who by good luck was standing there, noticed it and pulled it out with a hook, thinking that he had found a great treasure. But when he opened it there lay a pretty boy inside, quite fresh and lively. He took him to the miller and his wife, and as they had no children they were glad, and said, "God has given him to us." They took great care of the foundling, and he grew up in all goodness.

It happened that once, in a storm, the king went into the mill and asked the mill-folk if the tall youth was their son. "No," answered they, "he's a foundling. Fourteen years ago he floated down to the milldam in a box, and the mill-boy pulled him out of the water."

Then the king knew that it was none other than the luck-child that he had thrown into the water, and he said, "My good people, could not the youth take a letter to the queen? I will give him two gold pieces as a reward."

"Just as the king commands," answered they, and

they told the boy to hold himself in readiness.

Then the king wrote a letter to the queen, wherein he said, "As soon as the boy arrives with this letter, let him be killed and buried, and all must be done before I come home."

The boy set out with this letter, but he lost his way, and in the evening came to a large forest. In the darkness he saw a small light; he went toward it and reached a cottage. When he went in, an old woman was sitting by the fire quite alone. She started when she saw the boy, and said, "Whence do you come, and whither are you going?"

"I come from the mill," he answered, "and wish to go to the queen, to whom I am taking a letter; but as I have lost my way in the forest I should like to stay here overnight."

"You poor boy," said the woman, "you have come into a den of thieves, and when they come home they will kill you."

"Let them come," said the boy. "I am not afraid; but I am so tired that I cannot go any farther." And he stretched himself upon a bench and fell asleep.

Soon afterward the robbers came and angrily asked what strange boy was lying there. "Ah," said the old woman, "it is an innocent child who has lost himself in the forest, and out of pity I have let him come in; he has to take a letter to the queen." The robbers opened the letter and read it, and in it was written that the boy, as soon as he arrived, should be put to death. Then the hard-hearted robbers felt pity, and their leader tore up the letter and wrote another, saying that as soon as the boy came, he should be married at once to the king's daughter. Then they let him lie quietly on the bench until the next morning. When he awoke they gave him the letter and showed him the right way.

The queen, when she had received the letter and read it, did as was written in it, and had a splendid wedding feast prepared; the king's daughter was married to the luck-child, and as the youth was handsome and agreeable, she lived with him in joy and contentment.

After some time the king returned to his palace and saw that the prophecy was fulfilled, and the luck-child married to his daughter. "How has that come to pass?" said he. "I gave quite another order in my letter."

So the queen gave him the letter and said that he might see for himself what was written in it. The king read the letter and saw quite well that it had been exchanged for the other. He asked the youth what had become of the letter entrusted to him, and why he had brought another instead of it.

"I know nothing about it," answered he. "It must have been changed in the night, when I slept in the forest."

The king said in a passion, "You shall not have everything quite so much your own way; whosoever marries my daughter must fetch me from hell three golden hairs from the head of the devil; bring me what I want, and you shall keep my daughter."

In this way the king hoped to be rid of him forever. But the luck-child answered, "I will fetch the golden hairs; I am not afraid of the devil." Thereupon he took leave of them and began his journey.

The road led him to a large town, where the watchman by the gates asked him what his trade was and what he knew. "I know everything," answered the luck-child.

"Then you can do us a favor," said the watchman, "if you will tell us why our market fountain, which once flowed with wine, has become dry, and no longer gives even water."

"That you shall know," answered he. "Only wait until I come back."

Then he went farther and came to another town, and there also the gatekeeper asked him what was his trade and what he knew. "I know everything," answered he.

"Then you can do us a favor, and tell us why a tree in our town, which once bore golden apples, now does not even put forth leaves."

"You shall know that," answered he. "Only wait

until I come back."

Then he went on and came to a wide river over which he must go. The ferryman asked him what his trade was and what he knew. "I know everything," answered he.

"Then you can do me a favor," said the ferryman, "and tell me why I must always be rowing backward and forward, and am never set free."

"You shall know that," answered he. "Only wait until I come back."

When he had crossed the water he found the entrance to hell. It was black and sooty within, and the devil was not at home, but his grandmother was sitting in a large armchair. "What do you want?" said she to him, but she did not look so very wicked.

"I should like to have three golden hairs from the devil's head," answered he, "else I cannot keep my wife."

"That is a good deal to ask for," said she. "If the devil comes home and finds you, it will cost you your life; but as I pity you, I will see if I cannot help you."

She changed him into an ant and said, "Creep into the folds of my dress; you will be safe there."

"Yes," answered he, "so far, so good; but there are three things besides that I want to know: why a fountain that once flowed with wine has become dry, and no longer gives even water; why a tree that once bore golden apples does not even put forth leaves; and why a ferryman must always be going backward and forward, and is never set free."

"Those are difficult questions," answered she, "but only be silent and quiet and pay attention to what the devil says when I pull out the three golden hairs."

As the evening came on, the devil returned home. No sooner had he entered than he noticed that the air was not pure. "I smell man's flesh," said he. "All is not right here." Then he pried into every corner and searched, but could not find anything.

His grandmother scolded him. "It has just been swept," said she, "and everything put in order, and now you are upsetting it again; you have always got man's flesh in your nose. Sit down and eat your supper."

When he had eaten and drunk he was tired and laid his head in his grandmother's lap, and before long he was fast asleep, snoring and breathing heavily. Then the old woman took hold of a golden hair, pulled it out, and laid it down near her. "Oh!" cried the devil. "What are you doing?"

"I have had a bad dream," answered the grandmother, "so I seized hold of your hair."

"What did you dream, then?" said the devil.

"I dreamed that a fountain in a marketplace from which wine once flowed was dried up, and not even water would flow out of it; what is the cause of it?"

"Oh, ho! If they did but know it," answered the devil. "There is a toad sitting under a stone in the well; if they killed it, the wine would flow again."

He went to sleep again and snored until the windows shook. Then she pulled the second hair out. "Ha! What are you doing?" cried the devil angrily.

"Do not take it ill," said she. "I did it in a dream."

"What have you dreamed this time?" asked he.

"I dreamt that in a certain kingdom there stood an apple tree that had once borne golden apples, but now would not even bear leaves. What, think you, was the reason?"

"Oh! If they did but know," answered the devil. "A mouse is gnawing at the root; if they killed this they would have golden apples again, but if it gnaws much longer the tree will wither altogether. But leave me alone with your dreams: If you disturb me in my sleep again, you will get a box on the ear."

The grandmother spoke gently to him until he fell asleep again and snored. Then she took hold of the third golden hair and pulled it out. The devil jumped up, roared out, and would have treated her ill if she had not quieted him once more and said, "Who can help bad dreams?"

"What was the dream, then?" asked he, and was quite curious.

"I dreamt of a ferryman who complained that he must always ferry from one side to the other, and was never released. What is the cause of it?"

"Ah! The fool," answered the devil. "When anyone comes and wants to go across he must put the oar in his hand, and the other man will have to ferry and he will be free." Since the grandmother had plucked out the three golden hairs, and the three questions were answered, she let the old serpent alone, and he slept until daybreak.

When the devil had gone out again the old woman took the ant out of the folds of her dress and gave the luck-child his human shape again. "There are the three golden hairs for you," said she. "What the devil said to your three questions, I suppose you heard?"

"Yes," answered he, "I heard, and will take care to remember."

"You have what you want," said she, "and now you can go your way." He thanked the old woman for helping him in his need, and left hell content that everything had turned out so fortunately.

When he came to the ferryman he was expected to give the promised answer. "Ferry me across first," said the luck-child, "and then I will tell you how you can be set free." When he reached the opposite shore he gave him the devil's advice: "Next time anyone comes who wants to be ferried over, just put the oar in his hand."

He went on and came to the town wherein stood the unfruitful tree, and there, too, the watchman wanted an answer. So he told him what he had heard from the devil: "Kill the mouse that is gnawing at its root, and it will again bear golden apples." Then the watchman thanked him, and gave him as a reward two donkeys laden with gold, which followed him.

At last he came to the town whose well was dry. He told the watchman what the devil had said: "A toad is in the well beneath a stone; you must find it and kill it, and the well will again give wine in plenty." The watchman thanked him, and also gave him two donkeys laden with gold.

At last the luck-child got home to his wife, who was heartily glad to see him again, and to hear how well he had prospered in everything. To the king he took what he had asked for, the devil's three golden hairs, and when the king saw the four donkeys laden with gold he was quite content, and said, "Now all the conditions are fulfilled, and you can keep my daughter. But tell me, dear son-in-law, where did all that gold come from? This is tremendous wealth!"

"I was rowed across a river," answered he, "and got it there; it lies on the shore instead of sand."

"Can I, too, fetch some of it?" said the king, and he

was quite eager about it.

"As much as you like," answered he. "There is a ferryman on the river; let him ferry you over, and you can fill your sacks on the other side."

The greedy king set out in all haste, and when he came to the river he beckoned to the ferryman to put him across. The ferryman came and bade him get in, and when they got to the other shore he put the oar in the king's hand and sprang out. But from this time forth the king had to ferry, as a punishment for his sins. Perhaps he is ferrying still? If he is, it is because no one has taken the oar from him.

Briar Rose

A LONG TIME AGO THERE were a king and queen who said every day, "Ah, if only we had a child!" but they never had one. But it happened that once, when the queen was bathing, a frog crept out of the water onto the land and said to her, "Your wish shall be fulfilled; before a year has gone by, you shall have a daughter."

What the frog had said came true, and the queen had a little girl who was so pretty that the king could not contain himself for joy and ordered a great feast. He invited not only his kindred, friends and acquaintance, but also the Wise Women, in order that they might be kind and well-disposed toward the child. There were thirteen of them in his kingdom, but, as he had only twelve golden plates for them to eat out of, one of them had to be left at home.

The feast was held with all manner of splendor and when it came to an end, the Wise Women bestowed their magic gifts upon the baby: One gave virtue, another beauty, a third riches, and so on with everything in the world that one can wish for.

When eleven of them had made their promises,

suddenly the thirteenth came in. She wished to avenge herself for not having been invited, and without greeting, or even looking at anyone, she cried with a loud voice, "The king's daughter shall in her fifteenth year prick herself with a spindle and fall down dead." And, without saying a word more, she turned round and left the room.

They were all shocked; but the twelfth, whose good wish still remained unspoken, came forward, and as she could not undo the evil sentence, but only soften it, she said, "It shall not be death, but a deep sleep of a hundred years, into which the princess shall fall."

The king, who would fain keep his dear child from the misfortune, gave orders that every spindle in the whole kingdom should be burnt. Meanwhile the gifts of the Wise Women were plenteously fulfilled on the young girl, for she was so beautiful, modest, good-natured, and wise, that everyone who saw her was bound to love her.

It happened that on the very day when she was fifteen years old, the king and queen were not at home, and the maiden was left in the palace quite alone. So she went round into all sorts of places, looked into rooms and bedchambers just as she liked, and at last came to an old tower. She climbed up the narrow, winding staircase and reached a little door. A rusty key was in the lock, and when she turned it the door sprang open; there in a little room sat an old woman with a spindle, busily spinning her flax.

"Good day, old dame," said the king's daughter. "What are you doing there?"

"I am spinning," said the old woman, and nodded her head.

"What sort of thing is that, that rattles round so merrily?" said the girl, and she took the spindle and wanted to spin, too. But scarcely had she touched the spindle when the magic decree was fulfilled, and she pricked her finger with it.

And, in the very moment when she felt the prick, she fell down upon the bed that stood there, and lay in a deep sleep. This sleep extended over the whole palace; the king and queen who had just come home and had entered the great hall began to go to sleep, and the whole of the court with them. The horses, too, went to sleep in the stable, the dogs in the yard, the pigeons upon the roof, the flies on the wall; even the fire that was flaming on the hearth became quiet and slept, the roast meat left off frizzling, and the cook, who was just going to pull the hair of the scullery boy because he had forgotten something, let him go and went to sleep. The wind fell, and on the trees before the castle not a leaf moved again.

But round about the castle there began to grow a hedge of thorns, which every year became higher, and at last grew close up to the castle and all over it, so that there was nothing of it to be seen, not even the flag upon the roof. But the story of the beautiful sleeping "Briar Rose," for so the princess was named, went about the country, so that from time to time kings' sons came and tried to get through the thorny hedge into the castle.

But they found it impossible, for the thorns held fast together, as if they had hands, and the youths were caught in them, could not get loose again, and died a miserable death.

After long, long years, a king's son came again to that country, and heard an old man talking about the thorn hedge, and that a castle was said to stand behind it in which a wonderfully beautiful princess, named Briar Rose, had been asleep for a hundred years; and that the king and queen and the whole court were asleep likewise. He had heard, too, from his grandfather, that many kings' sons had already come and had tried to get through the thorny hedge, but they had remained sticking fast in it and had died a pitiful death. Then the youth said, "I am not afraid; I will go and see the beautiful Briar Rose." The good old man might dissuade him as he would; he did not listen to his words.

But by this time the hundred years had just passed, and the day had come when Briar Rose was to awake again. When the king's son came near to the thorn hedge, it was nothing but large and beautiful flowers, which parted from each other of their own accord, let him pass unhurt, then closed again behind him like a hedge. In the castle yard he saw the horses and the spotted hounds lying asleep; on the roof sat the pigeons with their heads under their wings. And when he entered the house, the flies were asleep upon the wall, the cook in the kitchen was still holding out his hand to seize the boy, and the maid was sitting by the black hen that she was going to pluck.

He went on farther, and in the great hall he saw the whole of the court lying asleep, and up by the throne lay the king and queen.

Then he went on still farther, and all was so quiet that a breath could be heard, and at last he came to the tower and opened the door into the little room where Briar Rose was sleeping. There she lay, so beautiful that he could not turn his eyes away; and he stooped down and gave her a kiss. But as soon as he kissed her, Briar Rose opened her eyes and awoke, and looked at him quite sweetly.

Then they went down together, and the king awoke, and the queen, and the whole court, and looked at one another in great astonishment. The horses in the courtyard stood up and shook themselves; the hounds jumped up and wagged their tails; the pigeons upon the roof pulled out their heads from under their wings, looked around, and flew into the open country; the flies on the wall crept again; the fire in the kitchen burned up and flickered and cooked the meat; the spit began to turn and frizzle again, the cook gave the boy such a box on the ear that he screamed, and the maid plucked the fowl ready for the spit.

And then the marriage of the king's son with Briar Rose was celebrated with all splendor, and they lived contented to the end of their days.

The Singing, Soaring Lark

THERE WAS ONCE UPON A TIME a man who was about to set out on a long journey, and on departing he asked his three daughters what he should bring back with him for them. Whereupon the eldest wished for pearls, the second wished for diamonds, but the third said, "Dear father, I should like a singing, soaring lark."

The father said, "Yes, if I can get it, you shall have it," kissed all three, and set out. Now when the time had come for him to be on his way home again, he had brought pearls and diamonds for the two eldest, but he had sought everywhere in vain for a singing, soaring lark for the youngest, and he was very unhappy about it, for she was his favorite child. Then his road lay through a forest, and in the midst of it was a splendid castle; near the castle stood a tree, but quite on the top of the tree, he saw a singing, soaring lark. "Aha, you come just at the right moment!" he said, quite delighted, and called to his servant to climb up and catch the little creature.

But as he approached the tree, a lion leapt from beneath it, shook himself, and roared till the leaves on the trees trembled. "He who tries to steal my singing, soaring lark," he cried, "will I devour."

Then the man said, "I did not know that the bird belonged to thee. I will make amends for the wrong I have done and ransom myself with a large sum of money, only spare my life."

The lion said, "Nothing can save thee, unless thou wilt promise to give me for mine own what first meets thee on thy return home; if thou wilt do that, I will grant thee thy life, and thou shalt have the bird for thy daughter, into the bargain."

But the man hesitated and said, "That might be my youngest daughter; she loves me best, and always runs to meet me on my return home."

The servant, however, was terrified and said, "Why should your daughter be the very one to meet you? It might as easily be a cat, or dog." Then the man allowed himself to be persuaded, took the singing, soaring lark, and promised to give the lion whatsoever should first meet him on his return home.

When he reached home and entered his house, the first who met him was no other than his youngest and dearest daughter, who came running up and kissed and embraced him. When she saw that he had brought with him a singing, soaring lark, she was beside herself with joy. The father, however, could not rejoice, but began to weep and said, "My dearest child, I have bought the little bird dear. In return for it, I have been obliged to promise thee to a savage lion, and when he has thee he will tear thee in pieces and devour thee."

He told her all, just as it had happened, and begged her not to go there, come what might. But she consoled him and said, "Dearest father, indeed your promise must be fulfilled. I will go thither and soften the lion, so that I may return to thee safely."

Next morning she had the road pointed out to her, took leave, and went fearlessly out into the forest. The lion, however, was an enchanted prince; he was by day a lion, and all his people were lions with him, but in the night they resumed their natural human shapes. On her arrival she was kindly received and led into the castle. When night came, the lion turned into a handsome man, and their wedding was celebrated with great magnificence. They lived happily together, remained awake at night, and slept in the daytime.

One evening he came and said, "Tomorrow there is a feast in thy father's house, because your eldest sister is to be married, and if thou art inclined to go there, my lions shall escort thee."

She said, "Yes, I should very much like to see my father again," and went thither, accompanied by the lions. There was great joy when she arrived, for they had all believed that she had been torn in pieces by the lion and had long ceased to live. But she told them what a handsome husband she had and how well off she was. She remained with them while the wedding feast lasted, and then went back again to the forest.

When the second daughter was about to be married, and she was again invited to the wedding, she said to the lion, "This time I will not be alone; thou must come with me." The lion, however, said that it was too dangerous for him, for if when there a ray from a burning candle fell on him, he would be changed into a dove, and for seven years long would have to fly about with the doves. She said, "Ah, but do come with me; I will take great care of thee, and guard thee from all light."

So they went away together, and took with them their little child as well. She had a chamber built there, so strong and thick that no ray could pierce through it; in this he was to shut himself up when the candles were lit for the wedding feast. But the door was made of green wood that warped and left a little crack, which no one noticed. The wedding was celebrated with magnificence, but when the procession with all its candles and torches came back from church and passed by this apartment, a ray about the breadth of a hair fell on the enchanted prince, and when this ray touched him, he was transformed in an instant.

When she came in and looked for him, she did

not see him, but a white dove was sitting there. The dove said to her, "For seven years must I fly about the world, but at every seventh step that you take I will let fall a drop of red blood and a white feather. These will show thee the way, and if thou followest the trace, thou canst release me." Thereupon the dove flew out at the door, she followed him, and at every seventh step a red drop of blood and a little white feather fell down and showed her the way.

So she went continually farther and farther in the wide world, never looking about her or resting, and the seven years were almost past; then she rejoiced and thought that they would soon be delivered, yet they were so far from it! Once when they were thus moving onward, no little feather and no drop of red blood fell, and when she raised her eyes the dove had disappeared.

Since she thought to herself, *In this no man can help thee*, she climbed up to the sun and said to him, "Thou shinest into every crevice, and over every peak; hast thou not seen a white dove flying?"

"No," said the sun, "I have seen none, but I present thee with a casket; open it when thou art in sorest need."

Then she thanked the sun, and went on until evening came and the moon appeared; she then asked her, "Thou shinest the whole night through, and on every field and forest; hast thou not seen a white dove flying?"

"No," said the moon, "I have seen no dove, but here I give thee an egg; break it when thou art in great need."

She thanked the moon and went on until the night wind came up and blew on her. Then she said to it, "Thou blowest over every tree and under every leaf; hast thou not seen a white dove flying?"

"No," said the night wind, "I have seen none, but I will ask the three other winds; perhaps they have seen it."

The east wind and the west wind came, and had seen nothing, but the south wind said, "I have seen the white dove: It has flown to the Red Sea, where it has become a lion again, for the seven years are over, and the lion is there fighting with a dragon; the dragon, however, is an enchanted princess."

The night wind then said to her, "I will advise thee: Go to the Red Sea. On the right bank are some tall reeds; count them, break off the eleventh, and strike the dragon with it, then the lion will be able to subdue it, and both then will regain their human form. After that, look around and thou wilt see the griffin that is by the Red Sea; swing thyself, with thy beloved, onto his back, and the bird will carry you over the sea to your own home. Here is a nut for thee; when thou are above the center of the sea, let the nut fall. It will immediately shoot up and a tall nut tree will grow out of the water, on which the griffin may rest; for if he cannot rest, he will not be strong enough to carry you across, and if thou forgettest to throw down the nut, he will let you fall into the sea."

Then the girl went thither and found everything as the night wind had said. She counted the reeds by the sea, cut off the eleventh, and struck the dragon therewith, whereupon the lion overcame it, and immediately both of them regained their human shapes. But when the princess, who had before been the dragon, was delivered from enchantment, she took the enchanted prince by the arm, seated herself on the griffin, and carried him off with her.

There stood the poor girl who had wandered so far and was again forsaken. She sat down and cried, but at last she took courage and said, "Still, I will go as far as the wind blows and as long as the cock crows, until I find him."

She went forth by long, long roads, until at last she came to the castle where both of them were living together; there she heard that soon a feast was to be held, in which they would celebrate their wedding. But the girl said, "God still helps me," and opened the casket that the sun had given her. A dress lay therein as brilliant as the sun itself. So she took it out, put it on, and went up into the castle, and everyone, even the bride herself, looked at her with astonishment. The dress pleased the bride so well that she thought it might do for her wedding dress, and asked if it was for sale.

"Not for money or land," answered she, "but for flesh and blood."

The bride asked her what she meant by that, so she said, "Let me sleep a night in the chamber where the bridegroom sleeps." The bride would not, yet wanted very much to have the dress; at last she consented, but ordered her young page to give the prince a sleeping draft.

When it was night, therefore, and the prince was already asleep, the girl was led into the chamber; she seated herself on the bed and said, "I have followed after thee for seven years. I have been to the sun and the moon and the four winds; I have inquired for thee and have helped thee against the dragon; wilt thou then quite forget me?" But the prince slept so soundly that it seemed to him only as if the wind were whistling outside in the fir trees.

When therefore day broke, the girl was led out again, and had to give up the golden dress. And since that had been of no avail, she was sad, went out into a meadow, sat down there, and wept. While she was sitting there, she thought of the egg that the moon had given her; she opened it, and there came out a clucking hen with twelve chickens all of gold. They ran about, chirping, and crept again under the old hen's wings; nothing more beautiful was ever seen in the world!

Then the girl arose and drove the chickens through the meadow before her, until the bride looked out of the window. The little chickens pleased her so much that she immediately came down and asked whether they were for sale. "Not for money or land, but for flesh and blood; let me sleep another night in the chamber where the bridegroom sleeps."

The bride said, "Yes," intending to cheat her as on the former evening. But when the prince went to bed, he asked the page what the murmuring and rustling in the night had been.

On this the page told all; that he had been forced to give him a sleeping draft because a poor girl had slept secretly in the chamber, and that he was to give him another that night. The prince said, "Pour out the draft by the bedside."

At night, the girl was again led in, and when she began to relate how ill all had fared with her, he immediately recognized his beloved wife by her voice, sprang up, and cried, "Now I really am released! I have been as it were in a dream, for the strange princess has bewitched me so that I have been compelled to forget thee, but God has delivered me from the spell at the right time."

Then they both left the castle secretly in the night, for they feared the father of the princess, who was a sorcerer. They seated themselves on the griffin, which bore them across the Red Sea, and when they were in the midst of it, she let fall the nut. Immediately a tall nut tree grew up, whereon the bird rested, then carried them home. There they found their child, who had grown tall and beautiful, and they lived thenceforth happily until their death.

The Valiant Little Tailor

ONE SUMMER'S MORNING A LITTLE tailor was sitting on his table by the window; he was in good spirits, and sewed with all his might. Then came a peasant woman down the street crying, "Good jams, cheap! Good jams, cheap!"

This rang pleasantly in the tailor's ears; he stretched his delicate head out of the window and called, "Come up here, dear woman; here you will get rid of your goods." The woman came up the three steps to the tailor with her heavy basket, and he made her unpack the whole of the pots for him. He inspected all of them, lifted them up, put his nose to them, and at length said, "The jam seems to me to be good, so weigh me out four ounces, dear woman, and if it is a quarter of a pound that is of no consequence."

The woman, who had hoped to find a good sale, gave him what he desired, but went away quite angry and grumbling. "Now, God bless the jam to my use," cried the little tailor, "and give me health and strength." He brought the bread out of the cupboard, cut himself a piece right across the loaf, and spread the jam over it.

"This won't taste bitter," said he, "but I will just finish the jacket before I take a bite." He laid the bread near him, sewed on, and in his joy, made bigger and bigger stitches.

In the meantime the smell of the sweet jam ascended so to the wall, where the flies were sitting in great numbers, that they were attracted and descended on it in hosts. "Hello! Who invited you?" said the little tailor, and drove the unbidden guests away. The flies, however, who understood no German, would not be turned away, but came back again in ever-increasing companies. The little tailor at last lost all patience, got a bit of cloth from the hole under his worktable, and saying, "Wait, and I will give it to you," struck it mercilessly on them. When he drew it away and counted, there lay before him no fewer than seven, dead and with legs stretched out.

"Art thou a fellow of that sort?" said he, and could not help admiring his own bravery. "The whole town shall know of this!" And the little tailor hastened to cut himself a belt, stitched it, and embroidered on it in large letters, *Seven at one stroke!* "What, the town?" he continued. "The whole world shall hear of it!" and his heart wagged with joy like a lamb's tail.

The tailor put on the belt and resolved to go forth into the world, because he thought his workshop was too small for his valor. Before he went away, he sought about in the house to see if there was anything that he could take with him; however, he found nothing but an old chunk of cheese, and that he put in his pocket. In front of the door he observed a bird that had caught itself in the thicket. It had to go into his pocket with the cheese.

Now he took to the road boldly, and as he was light and nimble, he felt no fatigue. The road led him up a mountain, and when he had reached the highest point of it, there sat a powerful giant looking about him quite comfortably. The little tailor went bravely up and said to him, "Good day, comrade; so thou art sitting there overlooking the widespread world! I am just on my way thither, and want to try my luck. Hast thou any inclination to go with me?"

The giant looked contemptuously at the tailor and said, "Thou ragamuffin! Thou miserable creature!"

"Oh, indeed?" answered the little tailor, unbuttoned his coat, and showed the giant the belt. "There mayst thou read what kind of a man I am!"

The giant read—*Seven at one stroke!*—thought that they had been men whom the tailor had killed and began to feel a little respect for the tiny fellow. Nevertheless, he wished to try him first and took a stone in his hand and squeezed it together so that water dropped out of it. "Do that likewise," said the giant, "if thou hast strength."

"Is that all?" said the tailor. "That is child's play with us!" He put his hand into his pocket, brought out the soft cheese, and pressed it until the liquid ran out of it. "Faith," said he, "that was a little better, wasn't it?"

The giant did not know what to say, and could not believe it of the little man. Then the giant picked up a stone and threw it so high that the eye could scarcely follow it. "Now, little mite of a man, do that likewise."

"Well thrown," said the tailor, "but after all, the stone came down to earth again; I will throw you one that shall never come back at all." And he put his hand into his pocket, took out the bird, and threw it into the air. The bird, delighted with its liberty, rose, flew away, and did not come back. "How does that shot please you, comrade?" asked the tailor.

"Thou canst certainly throw," said the giant, "but now we will see if thou art able to carry anything properly." He took the little tailor to a mighty oak tree that lay there felled on the ground, and said, "If thou art strong enough, help me to carry the tree out of the forest."

"Readily," answered the little man. "Take thou the trunk on thy shoulders, and I will raise up the branches and twigs; after all, they are the heaviest."

The giant took the trunk on his shoulder, but the

tailor seated himself on a branch, and the giant, who could not look around, had to carry away the whole tree—and the little tailor into the bargain: he, behind, was quite merry and happy, and whistled a song, "Three tailors rode forth from the gate," as if carrying the tree were child's play.

The giant, after he had dragged the heavy burden part of the way, could go no farther and cried, "Hark you, I shall have to let the tree fall!"

The tailor sprang nimbly down, seized the tree with both arms as if he had been carrying it, and said to the giant, "Thou art such a great fellow, and yet canst not even carry the tree!"

They went on together, and as they passed a cherry tree, the giant laid hold of the top of the tree where the ripest fruit was hanging, bent it down, gave it into the tailor's hand, and bade him eat. But the little tailor was much too weak to hold the tree, and when the giant let it go, it sprang back again, and the tailor was hurried into the air with it. When he had fallen down again without injury, the giant said, "What is this? Hast thou not strength enough to hold the weak twig?"

"There is no lack of strength," answered the little tailor. "Dost thou think that could be anything to a man who has struck down seven at one blow? I leapt over the tree because the huntsmen are shooting down there in the thicket. Jump as I did, if thou canst do it." The giant made the attempt but could not get over the tree and remained hanging in the branches so that in this also the tailor kept the upper hand.

The giant said, "If thou art such a valiant fellow, come with me into our cavern and spend the night with us." The little tailor was willing and followed him. When they went into the cave, other giants were sitting there by the fire, and each of them had a roasted sheep in his hand and was eating it. The little tailor looked around and thought, *It is much more spacious here than in my workshop.* The giant showed him a bed and said he was to lie down in it and sleep. The bed, however, was too big for the little tailor; he did not lie down in it but crept into a corner.

When it was midnight, and the giant thought that the little tailor was lying in a sound sleep, he got up, took a great iron bar, cut through the bed with one blow, and thought he had given the grasshopper his finishing stroke. With the earliest dawn the giants went into the forest and had quite forgotten the little tailor, when all at once he walked up to them quite merrily and boldly. The giants were terrified; they were afraid that he would strike them all dead, and they ran away in a great hurry.

The little tailor went onward, always following his

own pointed nose. After he had walked for a long time, he came to the courtyard of a royal palace, and as he felt weary, he lay down on the grass and fell asleep. While he lay there, the people came and inspected him on all sides, and read on his belt, *Seven at one stroke!*

"Ah," said they. "What does the great warrior here in the midst of peace? He must be a mighty lord." They went and announced him to the king and gave it as their opinion that if war should break out, this would be a weighty and useful man who ought on no account to be allowed to depart. The counsel pleased the king, and he sent one of his courtiers to the little tailor to offer him military service when he awoke.

The ambassador remained standing by the sleeper, waited until he stretched his limbs and opened his eyes, and then conveyed to him this proposal. "For this very reason have I come here," the tailor replied. "I am ready to enter the king's service." He was therefore honorably received and a special dwelling was assigned him.

The soldiers, however, were set against the little tailor, and wished him a thousand miles away. "What is to be the end of this?" they said among themselves. "If we quarrel with him, and he strikes about him, seven of us will fall at every blow; not one of us can stand against him." They came therefore to a decision, betook themselves in a body to the king, and begged for their dismissal. "We are not prepared," said they, "to stay with a man who kills seven at one stroke."

The king was sorry that for the sake of one he should lose all his faithful servants, wished that he had never set eyes on the tailor, and would willingly have been rid of him again. But he did not venture to give him his dismissal, for he dreaded lest the tailor should strike him and all his people dead, and place himself on the royal throne. He thought about it for a long time, and at last found good counsel. He sent to the little tailor and caused him to be informed that as he was such a great warrior, the king had one request to make to him. In a forest of his country lived two giants who caused great mischief with their robbing, murdering, ravaging, and burning, and no one could approach them without putting himself in danger of death. If the tailor conquered and killed these two giants, he would give him his only daughter to wife, and half of his kingdom as a dowry; likewise, one hundred horsemen should go with him to assist him.

That would indeed be a fine thing for a man like me! thought the little tailor. *One is not offered a beautiful princess and half a kingdom every day of one's life!* "Oh, yes," he replied, "I will soon subdue the giants and do not require the help of the hundred horsemen to do it; he who can hit seven with one blow has no need to be afraid of two."

The little tailor went forth, and the hundred horsemen followed him. When he came to the outskirts of the forest, he said to his followers, "Just stay waiting here; I alone will soon finish off the giants." Then he bounded into the forest and looked about right and left. After a while he perceived both giants. They lay sleeping under a tree and snored so that the branches waved up and down. The little tailor, not idle, gathered two pocketsful of stones, and with these climbed up the tree. When he was halfway up he slipped down by a branch, until he sat just above the sleepers, and then let one stone after another fall on the breast of one of the giants.

For a long time the giant felt nothing, but at last he awoke, pushed his comrade, and said, "Why art thou knocking me?"

"Thou must be dreaming," said the other. "I am not knocking thee." They laid themselves down to sleep again, and then the tailor threw a stone down on the second. "What is the meaning of this?" cried the other. "Why art thou pelting me?"

"I am not pelting thee," answered the first, growling. They disputed about it for a time, but since they were weary they let the matter rest, and their eyes closed once more. The little tailor began his game again, picked out the biggest stone, and threw it with all his might on the breast of the first giant. "That is too bad!" cried he, sprang up like a madman and pushed his companion against the tree until it shook. The other paid him back in the same coin, and they got into such a rage that they tore up trees and belabored each other so long, that at last they both fell down dead on the ground at the same time.

Then the little tailor leapt down. "It is a lucky thing," said he, "that they did not tear up the tree on which I was sitting, or I should have had to spring onto another like a squirrel; but we tailors are nimble." He drew out his sword and gave each of them a couple of thrusts in the breast, then went out to the horsemen and said, "The work is done; I have given both of them their finishing stroke, but it was hard work! They tore up trees in their sore need, and defended themselves with them, but all that is to no purpose when a man like myself comes who can kill seven at one blow."

"But are you not wounded?" asked the horsemen.

"You need not concern yourself about that," answered the tailor. "They have not bent one hair of mine." The horsemen would not believe him and rode into the forest; there they found the giants swimming in their blood, and all around about lay the torn-up trees.

The little tailor demanded of the king the promised reward; the king, however, repented of his promise and again bethought himself how he could get rid of the hero. "Before thou receivest my daughter and the half of my kingdom," said he to him, "thou must perform one more heroic deed. In the forest roams a unicorn that does great harm, and thou must catch it first."

"I fear one unicorn still less than two giants. Seven at one blow is my kind of affair." The tailor took a rope and an axe with him, went forth into the forest, and again bade those who were sent with him to wait outside.

He had to seek long. The unicorn soon came toward the tailor and rushed directly on him, as if it would spit him on its horn without more ceremony. "Softly, softly; it can't be done as quickly as that," said he, and stood still and waited until the animal was quite close, then sprang nimbly behind the tree. The unicorn ran against the tree with all its strength and struck its horn so fast in the trunk that it had not strength enough to draw it out again, and thus it was caught. "Now I have got the bird," said the tailor, and came out from behind the tree and put the rope round its neck. Then with his axe he hewed the horn out of the tree, and when all was ready he led the beast away and took it to the king.

The king still would not give him the promised reward, and made a third demand. Before the wedding, the tailor was to catch him a wild boar that made great havoc in the forest, and the huntsmen should give him their help. "Willingly," said the tailor. "That is child's play!" He did not take the huntsmen with him into the forest, and they were well pleased that he did not, for the wild boar had several times received them in such a manner that they had no inclination to lie in wait for him.

When the boar perceived the tailor, it ran on him with foaming mouth and whetted tusks, and was about to throw him to the ground, but the active hero sprang into a chapel that was near, up to the window at once, and in one bound out again. The boar ran in after him, but the tailor ran around outside and shut the door behind it, and then the raging beast, which was much too heavy and awkward to leap out of the window, was caught.

The little tailor called the huntsmen thither that they might see the prisoner with their own eyes. The hero, however went to the king, who was now, whether he liked it or not, obliged to keep his promise, and gave him his daughter and the half of his kingdom. Had he known that it was no warlike hero but a little tailor who was standing before him, it would have gone to his heart still more than it did. The wedding was held with great magnificence and small joy, and out of a tailor a king was made.

After some time, the young queen heard her husband say in his dreams at night, "Boy, make me the doublet and patch the pantaloons, or else I will rap the yard-measure over thine ears." Then she discovered in what state of life the young lord had been born, and next morning complained of her wrongs to her father and begged him to help her to get rid of her husband, who was nothing else but a tailor.

The old king comforted her and said, "Leave thy bedroom door open this night; my servants shall stand outside, and when he has fallen asleep shall go in, bind him, and take him on board a ship that shall carry him into the wide world."

The woman was satisfied with this; but the old king's armor bearer, who had heard all, was friendly with the young lord, and informed him of the whole plot. "I'll put a screw into that business," said the little tailor. At night he went to bed with his wife at the usual time, and when she thought that he had fallen asleep, she got up, opened the door, and then lay down again. The little tailor, who was only pretending to be asleep, began to cry out in a clear voice, "Boy, make me the doublet and patch me the pantaloons, or I will rap the yard-measure over thine ears. I smote seven at one blow. I killed two giants, I brought away one unicorn and caught a wild boar, and am I to fear those who are standing outside the room?"

When these men heard the tailor speaking thus, they were overcome by a great dread and ran as if the wild huntsman were behind them, and none of them would venture anything further against him. So the little tailor was a king and remained one, to the end of his life.

The Bremen Town Musicians

A CERTAIN MAN HAD A DONKEY that had carried the corn sacks to the mill indefatigably for many a long year; but his strength was going, and he was growing more and more unfit for work. Then his master began to consider how he might best save his keep; but the donkey, seeing that no good wind was blowing, ran away and set out on the road to Bremen. *There*, he thought, *I can surely be town musician.*

When he had walked some distance, he found a hound lying on the road, gasping like one who had run till he was tired. "What are you gasping so for, you big fellow?" asked the donkey.

"Ah," replied the hound, "as I am old, and daily grow weaker, and no longer can hunt, my master wanted to kill me, so I took to flight; but now how am I to earn my bread?"

"I tell you what," said the donkey, "I am going to Bremen and shall be town musician there; go with me and engage yourself also as a musician. I will play the lute, and you shall beat the kettledrum."

The hound agreed, and on they went.

Before long they came to a cat sitting on the path, with a face like three rainy days! "Now then, old shaver, what has gone askew with you?" asked the donkey.

"Who can be merry when his neck is in danger?" answered the cat. "Because I am now getting old, and my teeth are worn to stumps, and I prefer to sit by the fire and spin, rather than hunt about after mice, my mistress wanted to drown me, so I ran away. But now good advice is scarce. Where am I to go?"

"Go with us to Bremen. You understand night music, you can be a town musician."

The cat thought well of it and went with them. After this the three fugitives came to a farmyard where the cock was sitting upon the gate, crowing with all his might. "Your crow goes through and through one," said the donkey. "What is the matter?"

"I have been foretelling fine weather, because it is the day on which Our Lady washes the Christ child's little shirts and wants to dry them," said the cock. "But guests are coming for Sunday, so the housewife has no pity and has told the cook that she intends to eat me in the soup tomorrow; this evening I am to have my head cut off. Now I am crowing at full pitch while I can."

"Ah, but red-comb," said the donkey, "you had better come away with us. We are going to Bremen; you can find something better than death everywhere: You have a good voice, and if we make music together it must have some quality!"

The cock agreed to this plan, and all four went on together. They could not, however, reach the city of Bremen in one day, and in the evening they came to a forest where they meant to pass the night. The donkey and the hound laid themselves down under a large tree, and the cat and the cock settled themselves in the branches; but the cock flew right to the top, where he was most safe. Before he went to sleep he looked around on all four sides and thought he saw in the distance a little spark burning; so he called out to his companions that there must be a house not far off, for he saw a light. The donkey said, "If so, we had better get up and go on, for the shelter here is bad." The hound thought that a few bones with some meat on would do him good, too!

So they made their way to the place where the light was and soon saw it shine brighter and grow larger, until they came to a well-lighted robber's house. The donkey, as the biggest, went to the window and looked in.

"What do you see, my gray horse?" asked the cock.

"What do I see?" answered the donkey. "A table covered with good things to eat and drink, and robbers sitting at it enjoying themselves."

"That would be the sort of thing for us," said the cock.

"Yes, yes; ah, how I wish we were there!" said the donkey.

Then the animals took counsel together how they should manage to drive away the robbers, and at last they thought of a plan. The donkey was to place himself with his forefeet upon the window ledge, the hound was to jump on the donkey's back, the cat was to climb upon the dog, and lastly the cock was to fly up and perch upon the head of the cat.

When this was done, at a given signal, they began to perform their music together: The donkey brayed, the hound barked, the cat mewed, and the cock crowed; then they burst through the window into the room, so that the glass clattered! At this horrible din, the robbers sprang up, thinking no otherwise than that a ghost had come in, and fled in a great fright out into the forest. The four companions now sat down at the table, well content with what was left, and ate as if they were going to fast for a month.

As soon as the four minstrels had done, they put out the light, and each sought for himself a sleeping place according to his nature and to what suited him. The donkey laid himself down upon some straw in the yard, the hound behind the door, the cat upon the hearth near the warm ashes, and the cock perched himself upon a beam of the roof; and being tired from their long walk, they soon went to sleep.

When it was past midnight, and the robbers saw from afar that the light was no longer burning in their house and all appeared quiet, the captain said, "We ought not to have let ourselves be frightened out of our wits." Then he ordered one of them to go and examine the house.

The messenger, finding all still, went into the kitchen to light a candle, and, taking the glistening, fiery eyes of the cat for live coals, he held a lucifer-match to them to light it. But the cat did not understand the joke and flew in his face, spitting and scratching. He was dreadfully frightened and ran to the back door, but the dog, who lay there, sprang up and bit his leg. As he ran across the yard by the straw heap, the donkey gave him a smart kick with his hind foot. The cock, too, who had been awakened by the noise and become lively, cried down from the beam, "Cock-a-doodle-doo!"

Then the robber ran back as fast as he could to his captain and said, "Ah, there is a horrible witch sitting in the house, who spat on me and scratched my face with her long claws; and by the door stands a man with a knife, who stabbed me in the leg; and in the yard there lies a black monster, who beat me with a wooden club;

and above, upon the roof, sits the judge, who called out, 'Bring the rogue here to me!' so I got away as well as I could."

After this, the robbers did not trust themselves in the house again; but it suited the four musicians of Bremen so well that they did not care to leave it anymore. And the mouth of him who last told this story is still warm.